Sinful

Crossroads

Sinful
Crossroads

Gaurav Tanwar

Srishti
PUBLISHERS & DISTRIBUTORS

SRISHTI PUBLISHERS & DISTRIBUTORS
Registered Office: N-16, C.R. Park
New Delhi – 110 019
Corporate Office: 212A, Peacock Lane
Shahpur Jat, New Delhi – 110 049
editorial@srishtipublishers.com

First published by
Srishti Publishers & Distributors in 2017

Acknowledgements

"People people everywhere, not a single known…"

Unfolding my first inked pages, thanking a few people who made it possible for my imagination to come forth in ink:

Thanking almighty, who gave me patience when it came to writing. An imaginative experience that I have inherited from my grandfather's tales, who also used to write.

My parents and teachers, who taught me how to read, and most importantly, to write. Also their support in letting me undertake the journey and making me explore the nature, and each character of this book that reckons my thoughts every moment. Finally, I let them speak in the unfolded pages.

Then I would thank nature, which persuaded me to visualize its beauty and made me capture the wonderful views and its wide spectrum.

A special thanks to some of my friends with difficult names who were there throughout the journey and helped me in deciding the book title.

I would thank my editor Stuti, and Srishti Publishers who supported my inked pages and brought them out on a remarkable and successful note.

A special thanks to my friend Mayank who stayed by my side throughout the journey as a reflection, capturing these best moments with me.

Happy reading!

The Present

Applying Wisdom

We are a group of six in college, all from well-off families. In spite of having a good amount of pocket money and a promising future of getting placed well, we are not fully satisfied. Though I won't say that we wish to strive to achieve something specific, but yes, we certainly are on a quest. It might have been the boom in the startup industry, or the trust we had in each other, that initiated the discussion.

The six of us mates are known to the world like this: Gaurav (which is me), Deepak, Deovrat, Amit, Ankit and Tarunpreet (fondly called Sardarji).

Deepak is a photographer and is passionate about his work. He called all of us 'My Posers', except for me, as I don't like being photographed. I used to write. I tried to start writing a novel twice, but was not able to complete it. I am in the process of completing my third attempt. As against the two of us, the other four lacked any specific talent that I can share.

One day, I asked them about starting something on our own. If it turned out to be a hit, we could convert it into a full-fledged business.

Ankit: What exactly do you want to do?

I: See, let's start small and then focus on growing. Winter is around the corner, and students have started going to the tea stall behind the campus. We can sell sandwiches or bread rolls with coffee or something like that. We can sit down and think about it.

1

Yeah, everyone replied excitingly, but the irony is that no one ever talked about it after that.

A few days later, I was having what you can call a brainstorming session with Deepak on the phone.

The conversation went like this:

I: So, have you thought any further on the idea?

Deepak: Yes, I did actually.

I: Like what exactly?

Deepak: A momo stall.

I: Good, do let me know the details.

The conversation ended, as I didn't want to talk about ideas over the phone. And it was inspiring to see that ideas were not coming to me alone, but to my friends as well.

Deovrat was going to Indore. Me and Deepak went to drop him at the railway station. I needed to speak to Deepak because he was the only one amongst us who was sincerely thinking about doing something about the idea. After seeing Deovrat off, we came back to the car.

I: So what's the plan? Have you thought of doing something on a serious note?

Deepak: Yes, I told you about the momo stall.

I: Give me the details.

We have to do it. That's all I got from him. He remained quiet after that. I didn't prod him any further.

Deepak (breaking the silence): So please suggest how to go about it. I can't do everything alone, and nobody else seems bothered about it.

I tried to make him feel at ease and make him realize we were all by his side.

I: Forget that idea for now. We can do much bigger and better things. See, you take good photographs, so we can call you a photographer. And as I've told you, I write; so you can call me a writer. Do you see where I am going?

Looking puzzled, he gave it a thought.

Deepak: Yes, you mean to say that we can make movies!

Absolutely! I almost shouted, trying to hug him for reading my mind. He smiled, but within a fraction of an instance, he frowned, asking me how we'd be able to make it without any funds, and that he was only a photographer and not an artist who could turn a video into a movie. I put my hand on his shoulder and turned towards him.

I: Did I ask you to be a professional? In fact, I myself am not a bestselling author. I am not even a published one for that matter. Just chill, the plan is not to make us worry about doing things, but to make us excited and ready to go.

Deepak: That sounds really amazing. So will you please tell me what the plan is?

I: Making viral videos at first, then travel diaries and then documentaries.

He looked at me with eyes filled with hope. He smiled, then laughed out louder and louder. Well, that was a good start, I thought.

Next Day
After class, I rounded the boys and the five of us headed to the boys' common room. A senior sitting in the room was requested to leave as we needed to discuss something important and confidential. He obliged.

I made the guys sit on a round table, told them everything and asked for their approval. Yes, all of them approved with great enthusiasm. Deepak created a Whatsapp group at once, which was to be strictly used for business. Mr. Thapa, who was going to be our cameraman, director and everything else apart from the story writer and actors, was brought into the loop by Deepak.

So we began. I was late for the meeting and the guys had already completed the full script for the first viral video. I was only asked to jot it down as they dictated everything to me.

I wrote the whole story on the very first night and mailed it to all of my teammates at 3.00 a.m.

We made plans of how and when we were going to shoot, and we had to wait for Deovrat as he was one of the main characters of the story. Deovrat hadn't returned yet and didn't ask anyone what exactly was going on, though he was keeping an eye on us through the Whatsapp group. I wanted him to ask us about what exactly was being planned and hoped he would, soon.

I described my vision to each of my friends again. I asked them to visualise how big we could become, maybe even the biggest production house of the country, which may also lay footprints globally, because according to me, our thinking was different. We wanted to make documentaries which were going to inspire people with stories of those who struggled and overcame difficulties to achieve success. I was more than inspired to make every move of ours successful. I was sure that if we'd give our best shot with sincerity, then ten-folds of it was going to come back. Optimism, you can call it.

We had decided the name for our team. 'Da Tag' it was to be. It took us three days to decide the name, as we used to sit for its inception, and even after hours of discussions and going through infinite names, we were not able to finalise any. On the third day, while we were almost getting tired, Tarunpreet shouted so loud that it scared all of us. He didn't just shout, but also started dancing with the happiness at completing the task. We all were laughing at him and he was dancing like a crazy guy. Just then, a faculty member saw Tarunpreet and asked him to come to his office.

Amit: Leave him! Will you please tell us what it is?

Tarunpreet: 'Da Tag'!!

Ankit: Now what is that?

Ankit was furious as his suggestions were rejected the most, and to him, this suggestion seemed totally useless.

Tarunpreet: You can't reject it, I can even bet on this. It's nothing more than the initials of our names.

We analyzed it for seconds and started looking at each other, smiling with the acceptance of our brands' name.

Deovrat returned, and after filling him in, we planned our first trial shoot. After class, at the tea stall behind college, while sipping tea and waiting for Mr. Thapa, Deovrat said he needed to go home as he hadn't slept the whole night. Deepak thought I'd say something, but I remained quiet. He could leave, but it shouldn't happen again. This is the first and last day we are letting you leave the arena, I wanted to say.

We worked on the project whenever we got time. Deovrat, however, didn't seem to have his heart in it. He'd often try to leave, as he had one day after class. He said he needed to go for some urgent work, but we made him stop for the shoot. And yes, he stayed for the whole shoot till late in the evening.

The next day, we were to have a meeting to schedule upcoming shoots. Before the meeting, we went to look at our marks in a faculty's cabin. He was not there, so we waited for him on the couch outside his cabin.

Deovrat said, "See, let's finish the meeting fast so we can disperse for the day."

"Yeah, we'll go in a while. Wait!"

"See, if you guys want to have a meeting, then please let's do it now. And why the hell are you behaving like we are a multimillion dollar company?" Deovrat continued. He had forgotten we were waiting to check our marks.

"What do you mean? You are not doing us a favor by waiting here. And how dare you demean my vision? I am here for something bigger than a multimillion company," I said angrily.

Deovrat sat expressionless. I had never seen him being so illogical before. Deepak looked at me without saying anything, and Tarun,

Ankit and Amit kept looking into their phones. No one reacted, but yes, Deovrat was clearly hurt. I am sure he would have punched the face if it wasn't me.

"Okay then, I am leaving," he finally said quietly.

Turning his back towards us, he went towards the stairs, almost running.

Ankit asked me hurriedly, "Why don't you stop him?"

I didn't reply, though it meant the exit of one member from 'Da Tag'. Should I stop him, I asked myself. "You shouldn't," came the voice from inside. But why, I asked myself. "Nothing is above 'wisdom', and this is 'my wisdom'," pat came the reply.

It was my wisdom which asked me not to stop a person who was leaving on his own accord, because even if we had retained him forcefully, he wouldn't have given it his all. So I let him go.

Thanks to Baba Aliyanka, who taught me what not to do at a particular point of time.

Let me tell you about my short trip to the Himalayas. A few years ago, I had visited Uttrakhand's Mussoorie, Rishikesh and Dehradun. I will reveal why 'wisdom' is so important.

I should also tell you how and why I started writing this. It didn't happen with a plan, but with a nightmare. One night, I woke up in terror, my forehead all sweaty. It was the night that I dreamt that I had slipped and fallen into the Ganges. I screamed for help as I began to drown. At that moment, waking up, I thought of writing this about life-changing experience. I sat at my table, switched on my laptop and began.

The Plan

✂

There was still half a bottle of vodka to finish in Mayank's car.

"We should go to Mussoorie," he said.

I got confused, giving him a puzzled look. I don't remember if we spoke further about it. But yes, he showed up at my place after a few days to make a plan. It was mid-October and the two bachelors' plan was slowly taking shape.

Mayank told his parents that he was going to Dehradun for a project with his colleagues. But how would I lie to my parents? I decided to ask them for permission directly. I told my dad that I was going to Mussoorie with Mayank on the 1 November, and to my shock, there was no reply. I considered it to be his confirmation. To make it clear to my parents, I'd just need to bring up the trip at least twice a day.

Mayank, on the other hand, was facing a tough question. His parents couldn't understand why I was going along since we were doing our internships in different companies. So he made up a story that we'd be spending a few days in Mussoorie after his project is completed.

As the end of October was around the corner, I asked my dad for the money for tickets for the Dehradun Shatabdi. We did manage to get tickets for a train leaving three days later, thanks to Mayank's dad, even though we had to pay extra. I told my parents that Mayank had arranged the tickets, and to my surprise, it was a yes from their side with a question about the expenses that were needed for the trip.

Ignoring it, I headed towards my room to have a chat with Mayank about how much money would we guys need for the whole trip.

I: Dude it's me. How much money do we need for the trip? Tell me the approximate amount so I can ask for a bit more.

Mayank: Five thousand would be enough, I guess.

I: Are you sure? I mean, you know the stuff we have planned. Will it be enough?

Mayank: I am asking you to get that amount from your parents. We have more with us to have all the fun we want!

I: Ohh yes, but I think I will ask for six thousand at least.

I went straight to my dad's room. He asked me how much money I needed.

"I guess five thousand would be enough to live on for four days," I said hoping he'd give me some more. Fingers crossed!

On Wednesday, 31 October, I was very excited. I couldn't concentrate at work, so I stayed for just half the day and lied that I had to attend my cousin's wedding. I told them I needed four days off.

They bought it and I marched out of the office like a boss. I reached home early to begin packing. We had an early morning train and I was to stay at Mayank's place that night as his house was close to the station.

It was seven in the evening and my phone rang. Mayank wanted to know at what time I would reach his house. With my mother's help, I finally packed my bag after three hours. I then saved Mayank's number in my mother's phone, in case of an emergency. My mother told me that since my dad hadn't reached home from work, she would give me the money and asked me how much I needed. I replied cleverly that dad must have mentioned the amount. Yes he did, my mother told me. She said he had asked her to give me seven thousand rupees, but mentioned for you keep the two thousand separately. I happily told her I would.

Finally it was time to say goodbye. I couldn't wait to begin our journey. Four days of freedom awaited us. My mother bade me farewell with an advice to travel safely, stay away from strangers and eat healthy. I assured her I would as I waved at her. For a moment, I felt a little guilty thinking of the 'sins' we were going to commit, but that was what the trip was all about!

"Call me and let me know when you reach Mayank's place," she said.

"I certainly will. Bye!" I waved at her and left.

The Trip Begins

After I left home, my first stop was at a recharge shop where I put in some money into my phone. I waited for an auto rickshaw to take me to the metro station.

It was eight and I settled into a sharing auto, headed towards the Metro station. I noticed a girl sitting on my right. I wasn't able to see her face because of the darkness, but she seemed pretty from the eyes of my heart. I began to get restless as I wanted to talk to the girl.

I tried to make a move, but no, it wasn't successful. But then I asked her. "Hey, can you tell me how long it will take to reach the metro station?"

"Do you really not know how far the metro station is?" she replied.

I was stumped.

"May I know what you meant by that?" I said after a bit of hesitation. For the first time, I was feeling nervous.

"Yes, you are going there so you must know how far it is," she said.

"No, you got me wrong, I am not from this city and this is the only reason I asked you. I am from Dehradun, came here to visit my relatives. I have to board the metro till the Kashmiri Gate bus stand," I tried to make things clear.

"Oh really?" she smirked.

I became really curious, wondering why she was speaking to me in such a way. I tried to look at her but realised that she was trying to hide her face from me.

"So you are going to Dehradun?" She asked.

"Yes," I said but this time her voice seemed familiar. I suddenly got nervous, wondering if she was someone from work. I'd be in trouble then.

I kept quiet and so did she. By this time I was sure that she was someone I knew, and a feeling of guilt started creeping up inside me. We reached the metro station, but the curiosity to know that who the girl was increased. I tried to look at her while stepping out of the auto, but she was gone before I knew it. I quickly paid the driver and ran behind her.

"Excuse me!" I tried to stop her, but she didn't respond. To my surprise, she walked even faster. I ran till I was beside her and finally looked at her face. Yes, I was right, she knew me; and I too knew her. She was Ishana, my ex-girlfriend, whom I had dated a year ago for two months. We had fought and lost contact since.

I realized why she had been speaking to me in such a manner. She knew everything about me and she realized that I was flirting. As I was reeling from the surprise, she walked off.

"Hey Ishana!" I shouted.

To my shock, she stopped. I had to screech to a stop. She turned around and before I knew what was happening, she hugged me. I didn't know how to respond; it was too much for me. In response, I hugged her back. This was the best way to respond because there are very few chances like these in a man's life, where you get a hug from a girl without knowing the reason behind it.

She was tightening her grip on my back. I didn't know what to do as it was a crowded place. I was feeling sorry for her, but I don't know why she was getting emotional. This kind of behaviour was very strange from a girl whom you'd dated only for two months, that too an year back.

"Hey Ishana, don't react like this…people are looking at us," I said embarrassed. People might have thought she was drunk because it was a crowded place.

I finally freed myself and then noticed her tear-filled eyes. Now what was that for? I was again shocked and felt bad for hurting her. I wiped her tears. She wasn't able to control herself and I felt helpless.

"Let's sit somewhere," I said.

"Okay..." She looked around and suggested, "We can go to Mc Donald's or Pizza Hut."

"No, let's go to a quiet place," I said. She nodded.

I held her hand and we entered the gates of Heritage City, an apartment complex near the metro station. She followed me without saying a single word.

So here we were, in the society's park. It was quiet. A few elderly people were roaming around and a mother was playing with her toddler. Watching them took me back to my childhood. We sat on a corner bench under a tree.

She was on my left and I had managed to hold her left shoulder with my left hand going along her back. I looked at her face in the dim light. She was so fair and I remembered the first day when I had seen her in a party and had followed her till she had given me her number.

"What happened, why are you behaving like this? Is everything alright?" I asked.

She looked straight into my eyes. I stared hard. The moment seemed to have frozen and all we could hear was the rustling of the leaves of the tree in the wind and the voice of the toddler. My mind became blank and looking further into her eyes made me fall for her, for the second time.

This time, it was hard to control myself. I pulled her closer and our bodies touched. She didn't stop me, raising my confidence. Our faces were close and I leaned forward. My lips touched her lip; the lower one, I clearly remember. My eyes closed and her upper lip was held by my lips. She reciprocated and we locked in a passionate kiss.

I didn't have any idea what was going around me as I was lost in the moment. Had somebody come and stood in front of us, I wouldn't have sensed their presence. My right hand moved itself, I wasn't responsible for it, and it went to her neck holding it tightly.

I still didn't know what was going on, but I was enjoying myself, and guessed that she was as well. Continuing the passionate kiss, my right hand started going down. First, it rested on her thigh and then started moving upward, this time under her shirt. She tried to stop it in the beginning, but then relented, I don't know why. Now what was that? Was it really her breast? Oh yes, it was her left breast that was under my palm, I felt it by squeezing it gently. She started moaning which was making me horny. Yes, horny this time. Just then, something unbearable happened – my phone rang.

The magic of the moment was gone. I took my hand out of her shirt in a hurry and she too pretended she didn't like me doing that and brushed my hand away in a strange manner. I felt rather hurt, I must admit, as I knew she had been enjoying the moment as well.

It was Mayank. I called him back. He wanted to know where I was.

"I am at the metro station," I replied.

"You were going to leave at eight. How did you get so late?" he exclaimed.

"Yes, but I got struck in something. I met a beauty," I said making him jealous.

"Who is that?" he asked clearly surprised.

"I'll tell you everything when I reach in an hour," I said and hung up.

Putting my phone inside the pocket, I tried to look at her face, which she had turned away from the moment I started talking on the phone.

"Are you fine?" I asked turning her face towards me.

"Yes," she said, with watery eyes which were making me crazy.

I mean, why the hell was she crying now? I was sure I must have relieved some of her pain. Finally, I said, "I hope you are not angry about what happened?"

"No, but we shouldn't have done it."

"But why? We both liked it."

She didn't reply.

"We should leave now, you must be getting late?" I said.

She got up as soon as she heard that. It seemed like she had been waiting for me to say that. We walked quietly to the exit. I tried to hold her hand, but she didn't let me. That made me angry.

"Why are you behaving like this?" I asked.

"Am I behaving weirdly?" This time, she questioned me.

"Yes, you are! First you hug me, and then you kiss me with every bit of passion you have, after which you let me touch you and now you're not letting me hold your hand. Isn't that weird?"

She sensed the situation and took charge. She held my hand, which made me calm.

"What happened to you? Why have you been crying?" I asked.

"I broke up with my boyfriend today," she said.

Shit! That was the word that came to my mind at that moment. I felt hurt for a moment, but then I changed the way I thought. Her break up was a great thing that happened because god wanted me to have a passionate kiss, that too after a very long time. So I thanked god silently.

We reached the Metro station.

"Bye Gaurav," she said. That was it. Not another word after all that had happened. I started walking towards my platform. After walking a few metres, I looked back; she was walking towards her platform. Waiting for the Metro, standing there on the platform I saw her on the opposite one, but tried to look away from her.

I thought of asking for her number when we were parting, but then her strange behaviour ruined my mood. Well, sometimes it's good to make an incident a happy memory and just leave it at that.

I boarded the Metro and managed to get a corner seat. I took a deep breath, closed my eyes, and recalled the moments I had spent with Ishana. A sudden jerk and I opened my eyes. A short delay was announced. I took my earphones out of the bag and settled down to wait.

It was eleven by the time I came out of the Metro station. I called Mayank.

"Hey where have you been man?" he asked without letting me speak.

"I am here at the Sarita Vihar station; come to pick me up," I said, worried about the money I had with me.

He took five minutes to reach. His brother had come along. I reached Mayank's place and was embarrassed to find everyone awake, waiting for me.

"You must be hungry, what should I make for you?" aunty asked.

"No, it's fine," I lied.

"Beta, at least have something light if you are not that hungry. I'll make you a sandwich," she said.

She made me two sandwiches that filled my stomach. I was already on the bed with Mayank's brother, but Mayank didn't want me to get any rest, because he was patiently waiting to know all about my encounter with Ishana.

He made coffee for us and made me sit in the balcony to narrate the whole incident. He was laughing, trying to make as little noise as possible. It felt like I was narrating a story to a child.

"Your day was awesome brother," he said excitedly.

"No, only the evening was good." I laughed.

After narrating the whole episode, I begged him to let me sleep. I looked at his phone and it was 12:30 a.m. We had to get up at five in the morning.

"I am going to sleep, you do whatever you want to," I said entering the room.

I fixed an alarm for five in the morning and slept like a log. The last thing I remember was that he was calling his girlfriend again.

In the morning, I was rudely awakened by Mayank. He pulled my leg to wake me up. I kicked him on his chest and thought that he would leave me alone. But no, I was wrong; he started pulling my shorts, almost taking them off. I too started pulling them, though in the opposite direction.

"Why are you doing this to me, I mean what is wrong with you?" I shouted.

Meanwhile a familiar voice said, "Mickey, get ready fast."

Yes, it was his mom's voice. Aunty's voice made me reach out for my phone with my hand. It was 5:20 a.m. I jumped out of the bed in shock; Mayank was already ready. "Get ready fast or mom will kill us," he said.

"What happened to my alarm?" I asked puzzled.

"I switched it off," he said. Hearing that made me feel like punching him on his face, but I forgave him and focussed at the task at hand.

I rushed to get ready, cursing Mayank a hundred times. I took a three-minute shower and was ready in ten minutes flat. So it was me who happily showed the middle finger to Mayank as he had wanted me to be scolded by his mother. It was 5:35 a.m. and the taxi was outside, honking.

Mayank shouted, "Give us five minutes…we are coming."

Aunty wrapped the sandwiches she had made for us. I put my bag into Mayank's and then giving Mayank the bag, I picked up the packet of sandwiches and other eatables. I laughed at Mayank telling his mother that I had intentionally given him the heavier bag to carry.

The Trip Truly Begins

><

Now it was time to leave and we were saying goodbye to his mom. We touched aunty's feet and she in turn hugged and blessed us. We opened the door of the cab, but the driver was nowhere in sight, and the cab was parked in the center of the road. Mayank put in the bags as I looked around for the driver. I finally saw a figure sitting on the roadside, wrapped from head to toe in a blanket. I was not able to figure out even a single part of his body, except the hand which was holding a cigarette.

I walked towards him and cleverly asked him to confirm that he was indeed the driver.

"Do you know where this taxi's driver is?"

"Yes sir, let's go…it's my taxi," he said.

We reached the taxi, but now it was Mayank's turn to go missing. Now, where did he disappear within a few seconds?

Getting concerned as it was a dark hazy morning with the gloomy shadow of the dim streetlights on the empty road, I called Mayank. I could hear his phone ringing close by. I headed towards the tone's direction and yes, he was standing with his back towards me.

"What are you doing," I asked?

"Pissing," was his reply and I punched him on his back.

"Oh, will you let me piss in peace," he moaned.

We finally settled in the back seat, and the driver headed towards the New Delhi railway station. After a few minutes, the taxi started speeding on the highway, NH-2. There was silence except for the joyful sound of the breeze entering through the slightly open window. We crossed the Apollo Hospital and our driver jumped a red light. Mayank and I looked at each other. "Bhaiya, please drive carefully, there are traffic policemen around," I said to the driver, looking at him in his rearview mirror.

"It's okay sir, we give a monthly portion to the traffic police, and even if by chance somebody stops us, we won't get into trouble as our taxi service owner has very good contacts. So, don't worry."

Hearing him to be so assured, we felt that we were in a safe place. As I listened to the driver and saw how he was not at all worried about getting caught by the traffic police, I realized how corrupt our country was becoming. There is corruption in every single thing.

We crossed New Friends Colony and the driver took the slip road. I thought we had to go straight for the station.

"Mayank, are we going in the right direction?" I asked.

"The cold is unbearable, and you are worried about the road! He must be saving petrol by taking a shortcut that we don't know, you don't get worried," he assured me.

I made myself comfortable by closing the window, and closed my eyes to relax.

The next thing I remember hearing Mayank's voice.

"How can you snore that loudly?" Mayank said shaking me. "Get down we've reached," he shouted. Still half asleep, I tried pulling my bag by leaning towards the trunk from the back seat. I opened my eyes and looked out, but the station didn't look familiar at all. Everything seemed new.

I was wide awake now. "Where are we?" I exclaimed.

"At the station, where else?" said Mayank.

"Which station?" I yelled. My eyes suddenly caught sight of a board and I shouted, "This is Nizamuddin station, and we had to go to the New Delhi railway station!"

Listening to this, he blew his fist and kept the money back into his pocket. He had been about to pay the driver.

"Where have you brought us?" Mayank yelled at the driver.

"Your request was to be dropped at the Nizamuddin station," the driver replied.

"Have you gone mad? Are you in your senses?" This time it was me and I shouted loudly.

"Sir, don't get angry…this is what I was told by my senior. Let me call him and check. What are your train timings?" he asked.

"The departure is at 6.50 a.m.," I said looking at the big wall clock at the entrance of the station. It was 6:05 a.m.

"You are asking me not to get angry? Look at the time. We'll not be able to catch our train," I shouted again as he was calling his senior with a guilty face.

"My senior is not taking the call," said the driver.

"So what are we doing now? Are we going to sit here and wait for him to pick the call?" I said angrily.

Mayank was quiet but he began to move towards the cab and opened the door. The driver looked confused but realized what had to be done. He got in and started the engine. It was a quarter past six then.

"Will you drop us on time?" I asked the driver, though I knew he would.

"Yes sir, you don't get worried, we'll reach on time."

It was dawn and we finally reached the New Delhi railway station; the place where our trip was going to start. We had reached well in time. I began taking out the bags. The taxi was to charge three hundred bucks according to the deal made the previous night. I heard Mayank speaking to the driver.

"We had a deal for three hundred. The person who booked it told me on the phone last night when I made the confirmation," Mayank said to the driver.

"But sir, you see, I got you guys here, that's quite far from the place you mentioned," said the driver.

"Don't you make me angry. Are we mad that we would mention Nizamuddin instead of New Delhi if our train departs from here," I shouted trying to show anger.

"Sir wait, let me call my senior again." Saying this, the driver walked a few steps away for explaining the situation to his concerned senior.

"Sir, he wants to talk to you," the driver said, giving his phone to Mayank, which I snatched.

"Is this the kind of service you provide to your customers?"

"Sir, I am really sorry, I must have told the driver the wrong address because he asked me when I was sleeping," he tried to explain.

"That's not my problem. Tell your driver that I'm not paying him more than three hundred rupees," I said.

After a bit of arguing, Mayank gave him three hundred rupees and we started climbing the station stairs that would take us to the platform.

Start of the Freaking Train Journey

People people everywhere, not a single known.

"What's this man, where are they all going? It's not even festive season, then why is everybody in a hurry?" I said looking at the crowd inside the station.

"Let them go wherever they want. Let's go and look for our train," said Mayank.

We hurried towards the platform and entered the station at platform number 16. Mayank looked at his ticket and then at the huge digital board hung in front of us find that our train would be arriving at platform number 1. We'd have to cross all the platforms to get there and we were already running short of time.

"Come fast and just follow me," he said, climbing the stairs of the crossing bridge. I followed him like an obedient child.

After a three-minute run, we finally reached the platform. It was quiet. There was no train in sight. Taking out my phone, I realized that it was only 6:43 a.m. We had not missed the train. It may have gotten delayed because of the fog.

"Let's go and check," Mayank said.

"Excuse me?" somebody said as we passed a few people.

"Yes?" I asked.

"Is the Dehradun Shatabdi arriving on this platform?" the stranger asked.

"According to the ticket, yes, but I'm also looking for someone to confirm."

"Okay, thanks."

"Come on, man!" Mayank shouted as I was left behind, talking to the stranger. Mayank was asking a security person about the details. Yes, we seemed to be at the right platform, I gathered from their conversation.

In a few moments, the train chugged into the platform. Suddenly, a crowd appeared from nowhere to board the train. We stayed out and watched the scene in front of us. The pantry boys were getting ready for the journey, putting in the packets of food. People were unnecessarily struggling to get into the train together, instead of each one waiting for their turn, adding to the chaos. I reflected on how selfish people had become. They only wanted to get their own thing done first and didn't care a bit about the rest.

"Where are you lost, man?" Mayank patted me, bringing me back to the platform.

"Let's get in," I said picking up the bag.

"So which seat numbers do we have?" I asked.

He instantly replied, "Thirty-five and thirty-six."

We finally located our seats. There was a table that separated us from the people on the opposite side. We put our luggage on the rack above and settled down. Mayank bagged the window seat but he promised we'd keep exchanging seats. We wondered who would be sitting opposite us. In a few minutes, a family including a father, mother, and child along with an old lady, presumably the child's grandmother, settled down opposite us. Dashed were our hopes of meeting people of our age whom we could have chatted with. They took a long five minutes to settle down. The little kid seemed spoilt and wasn't listening to anything his mother was telling him. The husband and the wife began having a conversation while the old lady began mumbling with religious beads in her hand. The aisle seat adjacent to me remained vacant.

I looked at the old lady and my thoughts wandered. Is god really present? And if he is, can we make him happy by chanting his name over and over again, without thanking him or praising him for something he has done good in our lives? Though I myself believe in god, but this question sometimes confuses me, leaving me without any answers.

After thinking a lot about the devotee of god, I wondered where the family was headed. Why was the old lady going along? She didn't seem to be bothered about the others. Were they going to some relative's place or to Haridwar for a pilgrimage? I looked at the members as they settled down in front of us. I thought it would be fun to talk to the child during the journey, but he was annoying and kept kicking my pants with his shoes, in spite of his mother telling him not to.

The train started with a jerk, and I couldn't stop laughing as the child accidently fell off his mother's lap and stood on the floor. His parents glared at me while the kid seemed embarrassed. Mayank tapped my shoulder to ask me to stop. I did and proceeded to look out of the window.

6:52 a.m.: A person from the Shatabdi's kitchen staff, wearing a green t-shirt with 'Doon's' written on the back, came with a tray full of water bottles, distributing them to the passengers.

As I kept my bottle on the table, the child grabbed it instead of taking his mother's, and that made me angry. I took Mayank's bottle and showed it to him saying I still had one. I took his mother's bottle and this time laughed saying that I had two bottles now. His father smiled a little looking at me, and his mother said something to him in their native language after which he kept my bottle in its place as I returned his mother's bottle.

6:55 a.m.: A guy in the same uniform distributed newspapers. I chose a copy of *Mail Today*. I didn't really want to read it, so turned to

Mayank and asked him to tell me the headlines. He looked at me in irritation as his eyes were heavy with sleep.

"Will you please let me sleep?"

But I wasn't done annoying him.

"Why do you have to sit at the window seat if you're going to sleep?"

"Because I'm more blessed than you," he retorted.

I was going to reply, but the arrival of one of the staff members ended our conversation.

7:04 a.m.: It was the same guy with a tray that had some biscuits and sachets of sugar, tea and coffee. This was followed by a guy who got us hot water for the beverage.

The family got three trays and the child curiously eyed my packet of biscuits. I knew the correct thing would have been to give the child the packet, but I didn't want to give it to an ill-mannered child.

Suddenly, his grandmother seemed to have awakened from her trance. She picked up her tray and as her grandson tried to take the biscuit packet, she angrily refused to let him. It was very uncharacteristic behaviour of a grandmother towards her grandchild. The child ran to his mother who offered her tray to him.

What kind of a family was this? I thought to myself. The grandmother was not interested in her grandson's happiness. The father hardly noticed what his son was doing. I also wondered why the child didn't go to his father for his tray.

Oh stop it and mind your own business, I said to myself. I looked down at my tray and began to make myself a cup of coffee.

I finished my coffee and looked at Mayank, who had been asleep all the while. I shook him awake and he got up in shock, as though he was going to be kidnapped.

"You woke me up again! Why can't you let me have a single moment of rest?" He almost shouted.

"Hey dude, don't shout at me, else I'll get down at the next station, and then you can enjoy yourself alone," I warned him. "I only wanted to let you know about your tea and biscuits."

"I don't want to have anything, and please let me sleep now."

So much for being a little caring.

7:25 a.m.: There was a two-minute halt at the Ghaziabad station according to the announcement. Outside, there were a lot of people and it seemed like they all were waiting for local trains to take them to Delhi. The train started moving and a few passengers boarded it, but my adjacent aisle seat remained vacant.

Just then, the child's father stood up and started walking towards the coach's exit; maybe he was going to the toilet. This time, I noticed the child's mother – she was dark, elegant with a beautifully carved face, having deep eyes and a sharp nose. And I'm sure she was not older than twenty-five or twenty-six. I stared at her and realized she was quite pretty. She looked up and gave me a shy smile. Getting nervous and at the same time excited too, I raised my eyebrow and she smiled again. She looked at her mother-in-law to confirm that her crime had not been witnessed by anybody. I made the first move and handed Mayank's packet of biscuits to the child. He smiled and tore it open immediately. The mother seemed happy by this move of mine and I took the best advantage of it. While looking intensely into each other's eyes, I took my foot out from my slippers and touched her toes. She closed her eyes in response. It seemed like she was enjoying herself. Her son was still busy eating the biscuits while we were having our share of fun. We were touching each other's feet madly and she was closing her eyes from time to time, making me more excited. Just then, I saw her husband opening the door to enter the coach. I pulled my foot back and managed to gesture to her as well. She wore her sandals within a fraction of a second as her husband came and started reading the newspaper.

Did I really play with the feet of the woman sitting in front of me? For the first time, I had flirted with a married woman! Quite unbelievable it seemed, but yes, it had happened. I lay down on the seats and went off to sleep.

8:07 a.m.: I woke up with an announcement that we had reached Meerut City Junction station. A few passengers boarded the train, and this time, the aisle seat adjacent to mine seemed to be taken. A lady of around fifty came and asked me to help her put up her luggage.

"So how's the journey going?" she asked as she settled down. Was she asking me? I confirmed.

"It's going smooth," I said as she smiled at me.

We began a conversation as the train resumed the journey.

"Are you going to Dehradun?" I asked.

"Yes, and you?"

"We are also going there."

"We? Is this boy also with you?" she said pointing her finger at Mayank. I nodded.

"Are you going for some work or for a vacation to Mussoorie?" I asked.

"I am sure you guys are going to Mussoorie, and I am sad I don't have a boyfriend, else I would have certainly had some fun." She winked saying this.

I was speechless for a moment.

"Don't worry, I am just kidding. You are my son's age, so I can tease you. I am a doctor and am going to see a few patients in Dehradun."

"Okay, so that's the secret behind you and your destination. You must be a gynecologist?" I guessed.

"Yes, but how do you know?" She looked surprised.

It's my secret…I read people's faces. I looked at the woman opposite and she seemed jealous because I was talking to the doctor.

I turned to the doctor. "Don't get upset, I just guessed it because most of the gynecologists I've seen are women of your age." She laughed in a childish way that made me feel more comfortable with her.

8:16 a.m.: The same kitchen boy arrived with our breakfast trays. I asked for a vegetarian tray for myself and a non-vegetarian one for Mayank. The doctor took a vegetarian tray as well.

"Don't they get bored doing the same job every day, asking the same thing to thousands of people?" I said as the boy left.

"I'm sure they don't have a choice. That's their job and if they won't do it, their families will suffer," the doctor reasoned. She sounded so much like my mother; in fact, any mother who taught her child the lessons of life.

She further added, "This job is fun, in fact. You get to meet new people every day and serving food to somebody is considered as one of the best things a human can do." I nodded.

I woke Mayank up and we proceeded to have our breakfast. There was a cutlet packet, a small jam packet, ketchup, butter, and two pieces of bread in a silver foil. **After** we were done, Mayank stood up and kicked my calf so that I'd make way for him to go to the loo.

"Are you siblings?" The doctor asked. Every new person we guys meet together asks us the same thing. "No, we aren't. People say we look alike, but I don't know from which angle."

8:51 a.m.: We had reached Muzaffarnagar. A few people boarded the train and a few disembarked. The train started to move and I suddenly saw Mayank coming with a girl. Who was she? I was trying to look at her face, but was not able to.

Mayank suddenly turned towards me and so did the girl. Oh no, it was Priya, who had been my girlfriend two months back. Mayank had met her once. I sunk my head into my hands on the table like we used to do in school when asked by the teacher to keep our heads down. I am sure the doctor must have been wondering what I was up to. Suddenly,

I got a sound kick on my calf. To my shock, Mayank was standing with Priya, who was smiling looking at me.

"See, he was hiding from you," Mayank said pointing at me, making me angry and embarrassed at the same time.

"Is it, Gaurav? Were you really hiding from me?" Priya asked in the soothing voice of hers.

"No no, why would I hide from you! Rather, I am so glad that we guys have met after a long time.

"Come to my seat! I have two seats vacant beside mine," she said.

"Yeah, take him," said Mayank, "he keeps disturbing me. I need to sleep."

I wondered if it was a good idea. Would it be nice talking about the pleasant times we had together or would we end up fighting remembering the reasons for breaking up."

Not giving another thought to the situation, I stood up saying okay, and asked her to lead the way. The doctor looked at me and winked. I smiled back as I followed her down the aisle. Priya was sitting in the same row where we were, but was a few seats behind.

I: So where are you going, that too alone?

Priya: Going to Dehradun.

I: But why? You never had any connection with Dehradun as far as I know?

Priya: Yeah, I never had. But things change, relations fade and new ones begin…

That line seemed to be directed at me.

"… so it's a new relation with this city. My sister shifted there for her MBA, so I'm going to visit her.

I nodded and continued.

I: How are your mom and dad? I miss the times when your mother would shout at you because of me.

Have you gone mad? Why did you say this? I angrily thought to myself.

Priya: They are totally fine, and they ask about you too.

I: Oh really? What do they ask about me?

This time, I let my heart go and didn't bother about where the conversation was heading. Well, if it would make us emotional, so be it.

Priya: My mother has asked me many times where that friend of mine with whom I used to talk for hours on the stairs has vanished.

I: So what did you say?

Priya: I told her that he has gone abroad to study.

She looked a little teary. I wiped her tears without wasting any time and took her hand in my hands. I felt like kissing her, but I had to stop myself, remembering we were in the train. We both kept quiet, holding hands. She held my hand tightly as she used to in the past. She would always say, "I don't want to let go of these hands, and you just make sure you won't take yours away."

I: I remember everything. I know what you want to say holding my hands that tightly. Every word you said...every move of yours. The magical touch of yours that made me comfortable in every situation. The way I used to play with your nose, after which you always sniffed to make me smile. The way I used to kiss your eyes after which you gave that beautiful look I would die to see now. No doubt you were the best thing that ever happened to me, but maybe my whole life was not meant to be spent with you."

Priya: But why? I wanted you for my whole life, rather for my next lives as well. But...no, I don't want you back now.

I: I am more than happy to find you this strong...

Before I could say something else, she interrupted me.

Priya: And *you* are the only reason behind making me a heartless person.

She calmed herself and I tried to change the topic.

I: Let's not talk about our past anymore; we can talk about the beautiful future we'll have separately. Okay, tell me what are you planning to do next?

Priya: I'll continue working and will join a correspondence MBA course.

Meanwhile, I saw the lady who had been sitting opposite me going towards the coach's exit. I looked at her husband who was still reading the newspaper. Without wasting a second, I left Priya's hand and asked her to excuse me, saying that I had to go to the loo. Priya seemed offended, but I didn't really think too much about it.

Opening the exit door of the coach, I saw her going to the toilet. I turned to see if anyone was around, and to my relief, nobody was. She was just about to close the door, but I stopped her with my foot. She opened it with a puzzled face, but smiled when she saw it was me. She quickly changed her expression, trying to close the door, but I forced it open. I went in and closed the door shut behind me to find her staring at me angrily. I was frightened for a moment, wondering if she'd shout for her husband. But I stood my ground. She tried to move in the tiny toilet and I tried to take a step forward. Her breasts touched my chest. We were definitely getting aroused by each other. Our lips met and we were soon locked in an intensely passionate kiss. We kept kissing and touching each other when suddenly there was a knock on the door. It was her husband!

Instantly she pushed me against the wall and shouted something to her husband. All I could understand was 'five minutes'. I was suddenly very nervous. What if he came into the toilet? I would certainly be handed over to the police. The woman would never defend me. How would my parents react? I would certainly be thrown out of the house. I began to sweat profusely.

I looked at the face in front of me. She was taking a deep sigh of relief. She told me to turn around. I did and heard her pee.

She kept her ear on the door, trying to hear if there was somebody outside. She quietly opened the door and rolled her hand over my pants, driving me crazy. I couldn't stop her now, but as she stepped out, I locked the door and recalled what had just taken place. I finally tidied myself and made my way back to the coach only to be greeted by a fuming Priya.

"Where have you been? Did you really go to the toilet?" Priya nearly shouted.

Her tone offended me. I said, "I guess it's none of your business; you aren't my girlfriend anymore." As I said this, she started crying without making any noise, but the tears were dropping like a leaking tap. I cursed myself and tried to make amends.

I: Hey, don't cry please. I was just checking your emotional level. I just wanted to know if you have really become strong.

I said this because I didn't find anything better to say to make her stop crying. I sat beside her, holding her hand and wiping her eyes. I kissed her cheek and the old aunty sitting in the next seat gave me a strange look. Priya too was rather shocked by this move, but didn't say anything.

I: Are you fine now?

Priya: Yeah, I am, but why do you always hurt people?

I smiled guiltily, realizing how rude I was, to almost everybody.

I: I know I've been rude a lot of times…I'll work on that. Okay, I should leave, Mayank must be waiting for me.

I didn't know why I said this, and realised within a fraction of a second that I had been rude again. Leaving my thoughts behind, I stood up and started walking towards my seat where Mayank was still sleeping.

"So, are you back for me?" Doctor Aunty asked, making me angry this time.

"Please don't talk to me like that," I blurted out.

She didn't respond to whatever I said and started looking away. Well, there I was rude again. But this time, I didn't feel bad for at least I wouldn't have to talk or listen to her for the rest of the journey.

09:53 a.m.: The train had reached the Saharanpur Junction station and there was a twenty-minute halt.

I looked outside the window; it seemed like a big station with many people, and more vendors. I saw an ice-cream vendor and craved for a chocolate cone. But I didn't want to leave our bags unattended as Mayank was sleeping and the Doctor Aunty wasn't a friend any longer. I tried to ameliorate the situation between us.

I: Aunty?

She didn't look at me. I again tried.

I: Ma'am, will you please help me?

This time she responded, but just by looking at me.

I: Do you want to have some ice-cream? I am going to have one, if you want, I'll bring one for you. Could you please keep an eye on our bags till then?

She heard me, but said nothing. I decided to take a chance and stepped out of the train. I bought my favorite chocolate cone ice-cream and looked towards my window where I found Mayank angrily looking at me and gesturing at me to get one for him as well. And he wasn't the only one. Doctor Aunty's finger appeared at the window. I bought two chocolate flavored ones for both of us, and vanilla for the doctor. I took one cone in each hand and the third in my mouth. As I made my way towards the coach, tragedy struck. The cone in my mouth fell onto the tracks. Just my luck!

After I handed over the ice creams to Mayank and the doctor, I began to feel drowsy. Before I knew it, I had fallen asleep.

11:28 a.m.: I was awakened by the announcement that we had reached Haridwar Junction station where the train would stop for five minutes.

"Did the train cross Roorkee?" I asked Mayank.

"Yes, while you were snoring away."

I suddenly felt a tap on my foot. It was the young wife opposite us. They were getting ready to disembark. I guess that was her way of saying goodbye. I looked at her. I wanted to hug her for the last time, but that was not meant to be. The family began walking towards the exit. She looked back at me. How I wished she would come back.

I went towards the exit and watched the family on the platform. Suddenly she turned back and climbed into the train again. She gave me a hug and kissed me on the lips, not bothering about the pantry boy standing a few feet away. Then she quickly picked up a water bottle that she had left on her seat. That must have been her excuse to get back into the train. That was quite an end to the brief time we spent together.

I came back to our berth smiling. Mayank looked at me curiously. As I sat down, the doctor said, "You can sleep peacefully now. None of us will tap you".

"Tap you!" Mayank said looking at me with questioning eyes.

I was startled. How did she get to know that? Did the doctor see the lady tapping my foot? I decided to ignore them and closed my eyes again.

I must have woken up after a while, only to find Mayank missing. I felt someone tapping my shoulder. It was the pantry boy who had come for his tip. He smiled as I gave him fifty rupees and drifted off to sleep again.

I was rudely awakened with Mayank shaking me roughly.

"What happened, man?" I asked in shock.

"We've reached, brother. Get up fast and get our bags."

"Yeah, let's get down," I said groggily and stumbled after Mayank. We quickly grabbed our bags and got down. We bade farewell to Doctor Aunty who was waiting for someone to pick her, bringing to an end quite an eventful train journey.

@Dehradun

✂

The scene outside was the same as it had been at the New Delhi station, just smaller in scale. We got down onto a chaotic station with vendors and coolies vying for our attention. We trudged through the crowd and made our way out. What a relief that was.

We hadn't met Priya before getting off, so I looked around to spot her.

"Forget her," Mayank said, "we have better things to do."

I nodded in agreement as we made our way to the bus stand at the entry of the railway station.

We wandered around looking for a bus going to Mussoorie.

"Should we get tickets?" I asked Mayank.

"Yeah, let me go to the ticket counter," he said and started walking towards it.

I was busy looking at the people around. There was a person selling balloons and another selling different flavoured toffees. In the meantime, a bus came along and people started running towards it. Everyone, it seemed, was running towards it. I wondered where the bus was going.

I stopped, rather caught a person running towards the bus.

"Sir please let me go," he said before I could utter a word.

"First tell me that where this bus is going," I said.

"The bus is going to Mussoorie," he said and ran off.

So there were about a hundred people running to board a bus that had about forty seats!

"Run fast and get two seats, I have got the tickets," Mayank's voice boomed as he ran along with the others. I followed him but made him stop.

"You're not serious about getting into that bus? I certainly am not!"

"Just chill. I asked the person at the ticket counter. This is a daily affair. We have our tickets, so we'll get our seats. The ones who don't have tickets will stand all the way."

"Then why did you make me run towards the bus?" I asked puzzled.

"That was just a prank," he laughed. "It's going to leave at two, so we have more than half an hour to kill. Let's get some lunch."

We walked towards the exit of the bus stand.

We decided to ask someone about a restaurant. I asked a policeman standing on the roadside.

I: Excuse me, uncle?

Policeman: Yes?

I: Is there a good place where we can have our lunch?

Policeman: Yeah, we have a range of restaurants; you can find them in the new city. This station area comes under the old city.

I: Sir, we're looking for something nearby as we have a bus to catch.

Policeman: Okay, in that case you can check out CNC Restaurant, which is on the right. Look for Hotel G.P. Grand and you'll find the restaurant as you enter it. It's about two hundred metres away.

I: Thank you, sir.

"Let's go, man, he's given me directions," I said to Mayank who was watching an incident between a biker and a rickshaw puller.

There it was: The CNC Restaurant in front of us; we smiled at each other. As we settled down, I saw that CNC was an abbreviation for Chillies 'n' Chimneys.

After finishing our lunch, we hurried towards the bus stand. There were ten minutes to go, and to our relief, the crowd had dispersed. There was not a single soul struggling to get into the bus. We got into the bus and found our seats. There were three seats in our row, so we waited for the third person to come. This time, I had bagged the window seat.

"Where is this bus going? Picture Palace or Library?"

A man entered the bus and asked me.

"You are in the wrong bus; this one is going to Mussoorie," I replied.

He started laughing, making me feel like I had said something wrong.

"What happened, have I said something wrong?" I asked.

"It isn't your fault; you must be here for the first time. There are two bus stands in Mussoorie – Picture Palace and the other is Library. The two stands are on the opposite ends of the Mall Road, so I need to know." Saying this, he got down from the bus.

An old man with a wheatish complexion wearing rather shabby clothes settled down on the third seat. As Mayank had gone to get a bottle of water, and his seat was vacant, the man sat down on his. I didn't say anything, nor did Mayank when he got back and sat down on the aisle seat. I looked across at Mayank and spoke to him in English, sure that the man in between us wouldn't understand.

"We'll have to bear this man all the way!"

"Our luck," he replied.

Meanwhile, the man called out to a candy seller and proceeded to buy some candies from him. He asked for one packet of orange, one mango and one Khatta Meetha. Putting the three packets of candies in his pocket, he stood to take out his wallet from the back pocket of his trouser. Meanwhile, a white couple came and sat on the seats behind ours. Giving the money to the seller, he turned back to the couple asking, "Are you going to the Library stand?" in perfect English. Mayank and I looked at each other in surprise. A feeling of guilt began to envelope me. He was still talking to the foreigners and I was cursing myself for judging someone on the basis of the clothes they were wearing.

The bus started moving and my feeling of guilt increased with every passing second. We crossed Dehradun city and I mustered the courage to talk to him.

"Sir, is there a place called Library in Mussoorie?" I asked, just to start a conversation.

"Are you asking me?" he raised his eyebrows.

"Yes sir," I replied with as much courtesy as I could.

He described the place to me as I nodded.

"Are you also going on a vacation like us?" I asked.

"Well no, I have been living in Mussoorie for the last eighteen years," he said. I am a teacher; the Father of Waverly Convent School, a boarding school for girls."

I was surprised and so was Mayank. He certainly didn't seem like a teacher, and a father to add to that.

I offered some chips to him. He took a few from the packet and passed it to Mayank. I decided to ask him about hotels in Mussoorie as he had been living there for so many years.

I: Sir, do you know of any good hotels in Mussoorie?

Father: Yes, we have a good range of hotels, and they're cheaper as this is off season.

I: That's great. So does that mean we can find a hotel for less than a thousand bucks a day?

Father: Oh easily. I know a manager of a hotel, but the hotel is very old and you may not like it, though I can get you a good deal.

I: That's really nice of you. We really don't mind if we can get a room for six hundred bucks."

He took his phone out from his pocket and began dialling the manager's number. However, it was unreachable.

"We'll call him as we reach Mussoorie, it doesn't matter. And we can make our way to the hotel if you can tell us where it is."

He nodded.

He described the layout of the town. The hotel he recommended was very close to Library.

"You can see it once you reach there," he assured me.

@Mussoorie

✄

"Is this the Library Bus Stand you were talking about?" I asked as the bus slowed down.

Yes, it's Mussoorie, I said to myself as I saw the board that had 'Library Bus Stand' written on it.

"Yes, we've reached and that is the building we call the Library," the father said pointing towards an old yellowish building on the right.

"So can we go and read books in this library or is it just a name given to the building because it was a library ages ago?" I got curious.

"No, it's not open for everybody, but only for the members. It is an ancient building and was built in 1841, but its first floor is used as a library and the ground floor is occupied by shops. But if you want to see it from the inside, then you can go and spend some time there by giving my reference."

"That's great, I'll surely go there," I said excitedly.

The driver parked the bus and people starting getting down. As I got down, I took my phone out from the pocket and asked the Father to give me the manager's number. I dialled the number and when it began ringing, gave the phone to him.

Father: I am Father Timothy. I want a little help from you.

Manager: Sure sir.

Father: There are two boys from Delhi looking for a room. Do you have one?

Manager: Yes sir.

Father: That's great. So I am sending these boys to your hotel. Do charge a reasonable amount.

Manager: No problem sir, you send them, I'll take care of the rest.

Father: Okay then, take care. I'll come after a few days to meet you.

I asked him the directions to the hotel.

"Can you see that big white building?" he said.

"Yes, but is that the hotel? It seems like it's a big hotel," Mayank said.

You are right; it is one of the biggest hotels on the Mall Road, but it's old and its charm seems to have faded."

"Then why don't they renovate or reconstruct it?" I asked.

"This is the same story with every old building in Mussoorie... because construction is totally banned in the whole area."

"Why is that?" I questioned him again.

"The reason behind this is the degrading beauty of Mussoorie; traffic and pollution are big threats, so the government doesn't want construction to become another."

"Okay, so this is the secret behind Mussoorie being called the 'Queen of the Hills'," I said and Father Timothy nodded.

"Okay boys, have fun," he said preparing to leave.

"Do tell us the name of some places we should visit," I said.

He rattled off a list that included Kempty Falls, Gun Hill, Company Garden and Mussoorie Lake among others.

We bade him goodbye and thanked him profusely for his help. The two of us touched his feet and he blessed us abundantly.

"God bless both of you. My blessings are always with you. But yes, always remember not to belittle anybody till you know them personally."

Mayank and I looked at each other with guilt on our faces.

"We are really sorry for our behaviour; we apologize and promise you that we are not going to repeat it ever," we said in unison.

"May both of you reach great heights."

These words made me freeze, a cold breeze rolled inside my body making me tremble. The impact was way heavier than what I can normally handle.

"I'll surely make you proud one day and will make you say that yes, my blessings worked," I said. I didn't say these words on my own, and it seemed like an inner being had forced me to say them.

Mayank was rather surprised by my reaction. He held my arm and asked me if I was okay.

Father Timothy said, "I have faith in you, my child, and I believe in the beauty of your words."

"Thank you, Father. We should leave now, you too take care," I said lifting my bag.

"We should take the shortcut to the mall road," Mayank said after Father Timothy had left.

We went up this steep and narrow flight of stairs to the mall road. The climb made us hungry and tired.

"Let's get something to eat," I said.

We were in luck. There was a Café Coffee Day outlet on the opposite side of the road. We went in and after throwing our bags on a table for four, we rushed to the counter to order.

"I would like to have one cappuccino, and what are you having?" Mayank asked.

"An Irish coffee along with one samosa and a chilli cheese toast," I said.

The person at the billing counter repeated our order to confirm. We went back to our table and looked out of the window. We could see the city of Dehradun below the valleys. The view was breathtakingly beautiful. Our food arrived and we fell upon it hungrily. We ordered a few more items to satiate our stomachs.

Once we were done, we could really do with a nap, so we headed towards the Roselynn Estate Hotel. It looked like a castle. There was not a soul around as we made our way to the reception and I began to get a little scared. We met the manager who had booked us a room for seven hundred rupees a night.

He asked us to follow him to our room. We crossed the pale overgrown lawn which had two rusty swings. Entering the hotel's lobby on the right, he took a right towards the front end, but on the left I saw a towel hanging on a rope and some other stuff like a toothbrush, toothpaste, washing powder, and a few dishes lying there.

"Is someone living here?" I questioned the manager.

"Yes, the security guard, the cook and the caretaker," he said opening the room's lock.

I looked at Mayank and he was looking rather shocked as well.

"You didn't tell the number of rooms in the hotel and how many are occupied?" I asked the manager.

"There are forty-two rooms in the hotel, but this is the only one which can be used, I mean no other room is available for customers."

A big hotel with more than forty rooms and not a single soul except for the manager and the caretakers – I began to get nervous. Mayank didn't look too happy either. He went to check out the toilet while I wandered around the room.

"Are you sure we'll be okay all by ourselves?" I asked the manager.

"Don't worry, the caretaker and the other two will be close to your room. You just call out to them if you need anything."

He added, "There is nothing to worry about. It's off season and that's why the hotel is empty, otherwise you would have found quite a few families here."

We consoled ourselves and put our bags in the room. We locked it and followed the manager to the reception. We began chatting with him. According to him, people in Mussoorie were very humble and loving, and he was very thankful to everybody in Uttarakhand for maintaining the beauty of the place. He was mature and seemed to be an educated person. He told us he was a graduate.

I: Why are you not working with some company if you've graduated in arts?

Manager: I want to stay here. The love for my native land is most important to me.

I: But you can earn a lot if you work in a good reputed MNC.

Manager: I know, but I don't feel like leaving my family and land just for more money. I will not be able to cope up with the pace of a city. We don't have things to spend money on, but we have nature's beauty to soothe our eyes and hearts.

I: I really like the way you think.

Meanwhile, Mayank's girlfriend called and he went out into the lawn.

I: How many kids do you have?

Manager: I have two kids, a son and a daughter. My son is in fifth and daughter is in the second grade. In Mussoorie, we've some of the best schools of our country such as Woodstock, Oak Groove, and Mussoorie International.

I: Okayyy, thanks for this information. I'll keep that in mind when I have to send my kids to school.

I asked him about the hotel again.

I: Everything's fine, but we're a little scared about being alone in such a big building. As it's a new place.

I thought he would make me feel comfortable and assure me not to worry, but the opposite of that happened.

Manager: Though there's nothing to be scared of, you're free to leave if you are uncomfortable. There are many other hotels. I won't charge you even if you checkout late.

I was very surprised. It was as though he wasn't going to take any responsibility since he left at eight in the evening every night. I didn't say anything more and decided to change the topic.

I: I think we'll do a little sightseeing now. Tell me about some places we should visit on the Mall Road. Also the name of a good restaurant as we are famished!

Mayank joined us.

Manager: You can go to the Gun Hill. It's the second highest point of Mussoorie. Lal Tibba is the highest, but it's far from here. You can see the snow capped mountains and there is a ropeway to get to it.

I: Thank goodness there is a ropeway, I thought we'd have to climb all the way!

Manager: As far as a restaurant is concerned, Rice Bowl is one of the most famous Chinese restaurants in Mussoorie. We also have CCD, Domino's and Nirula's, depending on what you want to have.

I: Thank you. Hope we'll be back before you leave.

I said walking towards the exit. Mayank followed me and we used the shortcut to the Mall Road. I narrated the whole conversation that I had had with the manager.

Mayank said nervously, "Let's look for another hotel."

"Let's look for one now, and if it's better, we'll definitely check out from that hotel."

We walked around taking pictures of the beautiful sights.

An old beautiful building caught our attention. Hotel Kasmanda Palace, the signboard read. We were captivated by its beauty and began walking towards it.

"Let's stay for a night even if it's expensive," I said as we walked towards it. The slope seemed to be never ending. We were panting but the hotel appeared no closer.

"How far is it? We definitely can't stay here. Look at our condition!" exclaimed Mayank.

Finally we turned around the last bend to find the driveway lined with cars and taxis.

"What's this man? What the hell is going on here? It's full of people. And why are there so many taxis? Is everybody checking out at the same time? To make space for us?"

We looked at each other and laughed.

I asked a taxi driver what was going on and he told us that a film was being shot. Most of the cars and taxis belonged to the crew.

We continued walking towards the hotel. We were captivated by the beauty of the garden as well as the building.

"Can you see how beautiful this place is?" I asked Mayank.

'Yeah man, it is like a palace. Done. We are going to stay here."

"Have you forgotten the steep climb to the place?"

"We won't have to go out anywhere if we stay here," he chuckled.

Entering the hotel, we glanced at each other and appreciated the way it was taken care of.

Heading towards the reception, Mayank asked how much would a room cost.

"Sorry sir, we are completely booked for the next two months," he said, much to our dismay.

"How is that possible?" I asked surprised.

"There's a shooting of a movie going on and the actors along with the crew of the entire unit is staying here as well."

"Who are the actors? What's the name of the movie?" I asked.

"*David* with Neil Nitin Mukesh and Richha Chadda in the lead. They're usually sitting around in the lawns."

We were not really interested in seeing them and took our leave. We reached Gun Hill and checked out a few hotels there, but didn't find even one to our liking. We decided to get tickets for the ropeway. Mayank went to the counter, leaving me to check out some girls.

A face caught my attention – it was a fair and clean face, with nicely combed hair and brown eyes. It didn't seem Indian. Was it of some boy or of a girl? I thought to myself. For the first time in my life, I was not sure about a person's gender by looking at his or her physical appearance. The eyes caught me staring at them and stared back with the same intensity. I believed it was a girl, as she was staring at me, showing interest. I made a move by rolling my eyes upwards asking her to come up to the Gun Hill. She rushed towards the ticket counter.

Crap! What have I done? Was I sure it was a girl? Or was it a boy from some other country? Will I get in trouble? Is he gay?

We reached Gun Hill in our cable car. We got off amidst a crowd. There were shops and restaurants everywhere. People were looking at the snow covered mountains through telescopes.

"Which place is that?" I asked one of the telescope owners by pointing towards a mountain which appeared rather close, but seemed higher than Gun Hill.

"The tower you can see is known as the Time Tower, and the place is known as Lal Tibba – the highest point of Mussoorie."

"Can we go there?" I enquired.

"Yes sir, but you have to cross Landour, and you have to hire a taxi or walk all the way there."

"Taxi?"

"Yes sir, it's around eight kilometres from here and if you want to hire a taxi, then you can only hire it from The Picture Palace."

I suddenly saw the person with whom I had indulged in a staring contest. It was a boy! He looked at me before heading towards a small alley between the shops. As Mayank was busy checking out some earrings for his girlfriend, I excused myself telling him that I was going to the toilet. I went in the same direction the guy had gone. I spotted him and went up to him.

I: Hi

He: Hey, what's up?

I: I am great, you say? What's your name?

He: My name's Neithen and yours? Are you from India?

I: I am Gaurav and yes I'm an Indian, and you?

He: I am from Spain. Hey why were you looking at me like that?

I was not going to tell him that at first sight I thought he was a girl.

I: Yeah, I remember I was looking at you. You stared back as well. Anyway, tell me about your visit to India. Have you come alone or with friends?

I cleverly changed the topic.

He: I visit India every year, sometimes once in two years. My mother belongs to India.

I interrupted him.

I: That's great! You have an Indian mother?

He: Yes, I have an Anglo-Indian mother and a Chinese father. They met each other in England at some business meet.

I: So you've come to India with your mother to meet her relatives?

He: No, this time I've come with my father. We came to Dehradun to meet my father's friend and his friend insisted we visit Mussoorie.

I: So what you do in Spain?

He: I am a fashion designer. I work for Armani, Gucci and a few other brands on contractual basis. You didn't tell me to which place you belong and what you do?

I: I am from Delhi, and am pursuing engineering.

He: Delhi, that's great! I'll be coming to Delhi on fifth, and if you want, we can also meet.

We exchanged numbers.

I: So when are you going back?

I tried to end the conversation as Mayank would be waiting for me.

He: Day after tomorrow. I have a flight to Kolkata from Dehradun after which I'll come to Delhi on the fifth, though I have my flight to Spain on the same day. Maybe we can meet at the airport during those hours in between flights. And yes, I'll call you to let you know the timings of my flight. Also tell me how could I find you on Facebook...I mean your name?

I: Gaurav Tanwar, and I'll surely come to meet you. Okay then, I should leave, as my friend is waiting.

Saying this, I turned for leaving and found Mayank coming towards us.

Mayank: Is this the toilet?

Mayank asked pointing towards the toilet. I nodded and then introduced them. After Mayank was back, we swiftly went our own ways.

Mayank bought a few things for his girlfriend after which we ate some paranthas with a variety of pickles at a restaurant famous for them. While we were still eating, I caught sight of a board which said 'Kachalu Chaat'.

"Now what's that, man?" I said looking towards Mayank.

He looked at me saying, "Finish your parantha, then we'll try that as well."

We eventually went to the restaurant to taste the famous kachalu chaat. Finally, after doing all things touristy in Gun Hill, we proceeded towards the cable car. I turned and looked at Mayank who was standing behind me and found Neithen who was standing in the queue a few positions behind us. I smiled at him. We got into the cable car and marvelled at the scenery around us. It was nature its her best. The green valleys and the snow capped mountains in the horizon were a sight to behold.

We went back to the centre of the Mall Road where there were outlets of Domino's, CCD and Nirula's.

"Should we go to the Rice Bowl?" Mayank asked as that had been our original plan.

"No, let's go towards the Picture Palace and walk along the Mall Road. We aren't even that hungry," I said.

"Yeah, you are right."

As we walked along, we passed by a pastry shop named Casa Mia. The pastries in the display counter looked mouthwatering and the variety of flavours seemed endless. We walked into the shop drooling. Mayank asked for a chocolate truffle while I wanted a brownie with chocolate sauce. They were so fresh and delicious. The brownie was one of the best I've ever had.

We continued our stroll. Suddenly Mayank stopped in his tracks.

Pointing towards a restaurant named Sicoh Bar and Restaurant, he cried, "My wait for *daaru* is finally over! And you're going to get drunk with me."

"You bet I won't!

We laughed and stopped at a viewpoint, looking at the entire city of Dehradun below us.

"How beautiful will it look at night!" I exclaimed. We crossed the old Central Methodist Church and a few yards later, stopped at the a sweet shop named 'Inder's Bengali Sweet Shop (since 1930)'. We loved sweets, so it was natural that we'd step in.

"Uncle, please tell us which sweet is the best," I asked the fifty-something man at the counter.

"They're all equally good. Try any you like."

We sat at a table and ordered two gulab jamuns. Piping hot, they were delicious. We quickly gobbled two more.

"Let's try the rasgullas," I said and soon we had eaten two each of the white syrupy sweet.

We looked at the display counter and decided to taste a piece of barfi as there was space for just that in our tummies. We asked for the bill and were shocked when we saw that the amount was close to two hundred rupees. The prices of the sweets were exorbitant and the man had even charged us for the barfi we had tasted. We felt cheated and left the shop with a bad taste in our mouths.

Stepping out on the road, I was amused to see Mayank smiling at me like a small boy in utmost happiness pointing towards a small shop on the other side of the road. 'English Wine Shop' the board read.

Mayank said in glee, "We'll get a bottle from here in the evening and won't have to waste money at a bar. I smiled at his excitement as we continued walking. Our next stop was for some jalebis at a small shop outside the wine shop. The man was frying them in a huge *kadhai*. We asked for two plates, but refused the rabri that went with it. Not such a good idea, as the jalebis by themselves were not that great. As we reached Picture Palace, we found a nice restaurant called Tavern and decided to have dinner there.

Picture Palace had a 5D CineBlast, a scary house, a gaming zone and a bumping cars area. We decided to get tickets for the gaming zone, especially to play Air Hockey. As I was standing in the queue while Mayank waited for me, my attention was grabbed by a beautiful girl who was standing two positions ahead of me. Wearing a pair of blue jeans and a white jacket, she looked stunning. She seemed to be a localite. I was not able to get my eyes off her face. She had big brown eyes and a pierced long nose, which was red maybe due to the cold as she was continuously wiping her nose with a hanky. Her nicely shaped jawline made her thin lips look more beautiful. And I fell in love with the grudged pony of her curly hair. As her turn came, she asked for two tickets for Bumping Cars. She left and walked up to another girl who had been waiting for her. My turn came and I asked for two tickets for Bumping Cars as well.

I went to Mayank and lied.

"Brother, there aren't any tickets left for the Gaming Zone, so I bought two for the Bumping Cars." Mayank nodded as we walked towards the cars.

I got into my red car and hit Mayank's blue one from the back and was thrown a volley of abuses in response. I couldn't believe our luck. There were just the four of us in the arena. I decided to go and bump my car into the girl's. But it had to look unintentional. I pretended to be an amateur who didn't know how to handle the cars.

I hit her in the centre, making her black bumper hit the wall. She turned and looked at me and I looked at her apologetically. She smiled when she realized that it was by accident. Little did she know. I turned around to see Mayank coming towards me.

"So this was the reason why you got these tickets instead of the ones for the gaming zone?" He teased me.

I smiled trying to ignore him and accelerated my car.

I smiled at the girl and she smiled back. I took a u-turn.

"So what's your name?" I asked.

"Shemona, and yours?"

"Gaurav. So, are you from here?"

"What do you think?" She teased.

"Your beauty certainly resembles the beauty of Mussoorie."

She blushed.

"Yes, you are right. I am from here, basically from Landour. I'm studying engineering from Dehradun."

I almost shouted, "That's amazing, and coincidently, I am an engineering student as well."

"Great, which stream?" She asked.

"Mechanical, third year and you?"

"IT. Second year."

"That's great…you are one year junior to me."

This time, Mayank made a sharp turn touching my bumper, giving me an angry stare.

"Is she your friend?" I asked about the other girl.

"Yeah," she said calling her towards us.

I called Mayank. Both of them came from opposite ends and hit our bumpers in the middle. And, instead of thinking about myself, I caught Shemona's hand, pulling her a little towards me. We all had a hearty laugh.

"She is Iyana, my college friend. She is from Nainital," Shemona introduced her.

"He's Mayank and we both are from Delhi," I said.

"That's great, we all are engineers and Iyana, they are in the third year and are our seniors. We should address them as 'sir'. You are also in the same year, right?" Shemona asked Mayank.

Mayank nodded.

We drove around after that. Shemona and I were having a great time trying to bump into each other.

"Are you really a learner?" she asked me with a raised eyebrow.

I laughed saying, "Your beauty has made me forget everything, even the way I drive."

After we were done, I decided to ask her for her number. As we stepped out onto the road, a man of about forty-five put his hand on Shemona's shoulder. I assumed it was her father and smiled at him.

He completely ignored me. Shemona had stiffened and I realized she couldn't even talk to us now.

Was her father that strict?

I looked at her and shrugged my shoulders. Well a small place was a small place, after all. Some things were simply not done.

"I feel bad for you," laughed Mayank as we walked back along the Mall Road. I looked at the crowd, and could almost feel the slow pace of life.

I peeped into a shop and found a man of about sixty sitting idle and looking out to the valley opposite the road. I entered the shop as he seemed to be someone possessing a vast knowledge about life. He'd certainly answer my questions.

I: Hello uncle, how are you?

Old man: Good and you?

I: I am great. Is this your home town or you just do business here?

Old man: I've lived in these mountains for sixty-four years. This is my ancestral showroom of jackets set up by my grandfather.

Meanwhile, Mayank was trying on a few jackets.

I: So, do you exclusively sell leather jackets?

Old man: No, we have a variety, including fur and woollen jackets, but we display them only when winter comes.

I: Winters! Which month are you talking about? The cold is unbearable even now.

He laughed.

Old man: It hasn't even started, my child. It is summer now.

I: Okay, but don't you people feel alone in this slow-paced life of Mussoorie? At least in the winters?

Old man: People here don't really feel alone, but sometimes, I do feel lonely.

I: What exactly do you mean by that?

Old man: Well, let it be a secret, because if I start, then I am sure the evening will turn into morning!

Getting curious about this old man's life, I wondered what could he have done? Had he really done something which he is still referring to as a secret?

I: Well, I would feel blessed to hear some amazing experiences of life from an experienced person like you. It would be a privilege.

Old man: I am happy that you are respecting an old man like me as we don't have people of your age respecting oldies anymore.

What exactly was he trying to say? His constant gaze made me realize that he was trying to get me interested about his past.

I: I am interested in learning about your experiences of life because it would certainly show me different ways to lead mine. And you must be having other businesses as well, I guess from your appearance.

Old man: Well, my son has different businesses and we own fourteen stores on this same road. I look after the stores and he handles the rest.

Interrupting him, I inquired.

I: Your son? You don't help him?

Old man: I retired from my services a few years back.

I: How many members do you have in your family?

Old man: We live in Landour, and I have a loving wife since the last forty-eight years. I also have a son and his wife. Their daughter is pursuing engineering.

I: So you got married pretty early, I guess.

Old man: Yeah, I was sixteen, and she was nine.

I: Nine!

I hadn't realised how loud I had been till I saw Mayank running in shock to us.

I: Didn't your family get caught by the police because of your child marriage?

He again laughed loudly. It was so infectious that we both joined him.

I: So you were telling me about your family and your secrets.

I stressed on the word 'secret' intentionally.

I: How is your granddaughter already in college?

Old man: As you know, I was married when I was very young and so did my son. That's why I have a nineteen-year old-granddaughter.

She was nineteen and that made me happy, as I was twenty. I don't really know why a feeling of happiness overcame me even though I didn't know her. I wanted to meet her, so I was trying to think of a strong excuse.

I: You said you take care of these stores on the Mall Road and the rest is taken care of by your son. I mean, what's this 'rest'?

Old man: My son is a politician in this area and we have a big catering business.

Politician! I looked at Mayank in total shock. Forget the girl, I thought!

I: Don't you work with him in the field?

Old man: I told you, I retired from work but the only reason I sit here is because I like meeting people like you and sharing stories and experiences.

The book *Tuesdays with Morrie* came to my mind and I remembered the phrase 'sharing experiences of life.' In the book, a teacher named Morrie shares his all-time experiences with one of his former students till his last day.

Meanwhile, Mayank joined the conversation.

Mayank: Does that mean tonight we will have dinner with one of the richest men of Mussoorie?

How could he invite himself to a stranger's place? I looked at Mayank, surprised.

Meanwhile, the Old man laughed and called someone on the phone and told the person to make dinner for two guests of his.

I: Sir...Sir, he was just kidding.

Old man: But I am not.

Mayank: Sir, please don't get me wrong...I was seriously kidding. We'll have dinner on the Mall Road.

Old man: I want your jolly company tonight.

This time, he made it clear that we were certainly having dinner with him.

I: Okay, if you've made up your mind, then we won't let you down. So now we have the whole evening together and I am sure that you are going to reveal your secrets.

Old man: I certainly will, but you've to make some promises to me. You won't reveal them to anybody. At least not here, and won't blackmail me in front of my wife over dinner.

Listening to his promises, Mayank and I laughed.

I: But what are the things that you've kept hidden from your wife?

Old man: It's what I did when I was your age. And please don't think you are here to laugh and enjoy my secrets; you also have to tell me yours. So I can gather the difference in our attitudes. I've never spoken about this with anybody but you, because during my college days, I was also a travel freak just like you guys. You must have seen me smiling when you entered. You reminded me of myself in the mid-seventies. I had a friend too, and the two of us were partners in all kinds of crimes.

Oh my god! This time, the coincidence was on my part. I kept quiet, but an ocean of thoughts leaped in my mind, leaving me speechless. He's using exactly the same words as I did. Crime.

I: Sir, should we start?

He asked Shambhu (his storekeeper) to leave and go to their next store.

Old man: Let me guess, you guys are from Delhi?

I: Yes, we are from Delhi.

Old man: A person from Delhi is somebody I can have a heart to heart conversation with because Delhi was the city where I spent four years.

Mayank: Yeah, carry on.

I: So where do we start? I mean which road, bus stop or railway station?

We chuckled together.

Old man: It was October 1969. I was nineteen and had shifted to Delhi to study engineering.

"Engineering!" Mayank shouted, making me and the old man jump.

Old man: Why, can't I be an engineer?

I: No, I mean we are also engineers, so he was surprised by the coincidence. So are you going to acquaint us to the Delhi of the seventies?

Old man: You just listen, my friend, and I am sure you'll be stunned by the things I've done in those days… and I am sure some of them would be exactly the same things you are doing. I was extremely excited about going to Delhi.

He winked at us.

…and super excited was my dad who was longing to call me an engineer. As you know, I was married, so it was a little tough for me to stay away from home. After all, I was the father of a son and had my responsibilities. The major problem was that my son was weaker than a normal child and I was not allowed to visit home more than four times a year; it was a rule in my college to make the students live a disciplined life. I had to leave home and my father gave me a sense of assurance as he was better at taking care than me. So I left home to become an engineer. A power plant engineer.

I: Power plant!

Old man: Yes, what happened?

I: Nothing, it's my favourite subject.

Old man: Ahhh…

He continued.

It was the first semester and I hadn't got a room in the hostel. I had to live in a rented floor in New Friends Colony. I was living in a very rich man's house who had one beautiful daughter. I was excited about starting my college life. The only reason why I rented the place was because of the beautiful smile the girl gave me when I came to enquire about the place.

She was a student of Delhi University, studying English Hons. Second year, a year elder to me. We shared a 'hi' at the bus stop every morning. There came a day when I asked her name after greeting her, and she said Anamika, asking my name in return. And this was the starting of our endless conversations.

I was so happy about the change that came in my life. I was so happy being her friend.

Let me clear my ears as he said 'being her friend'. They took things really slow compared to our generation. Instead of making her his girlfriend, he just thought of being her friend.

Within a week, we started going together till the bus stop. I was introduced to her mom who was similar to my granddaughter rather than my own mother. She used to wear jeans and t-shirts in those days.

The five minute walk to the bus stand became a twenty minute one. We used to talk about our lives, particularly about our college lives. We started missing a few buses, just to spend a little more time with each other. Our talks got personal, but I never told her about my wife and son. I started having my breakfast and dinner with them when her father was not there, as her father was a rich Mumbai-based businessman. Most of the time, he was not home, and she told me about him and his routine. He had visited them only twice since they'd shifted to Delhi.

'This time, he made it clear that he's going to visit us after three months.'

Grasping her unreadable look, I tried to clear my thoughts, 'So are you happy as you don't have much supervision?' I asked.

'Yeah, a little bit, but then he doesn't bother me, so it's fine. On the other hand, it's also sad, because I don't get any gifts.'

'So that means you like gifts?' I interrupted.

'Obviously, every girl does. Haven't you given any to your girlfriend?'

'I don't have a girlfriend, I was in a boy's school and girls don't usually study in my town.' I cleared her doubt in one shot.

'Don't you have a sister?' She tried to make it difficult for me.

But again I had a simple answer: 'I do have one, but she studied till the eight standard and was forced to leave her studies, after which she was married off within a year.'

'But why? Didn't you stop them?'

'I was small and was not allowed to interfere in the decisions taken by my father. The other thing was the temperament of the people there. They believed in this, so we had to follow the norms of the society.'

After this heated conversation, she tried to ignore me for a week.

Mayank and I patiently listened to him. Though I didn't know what Mayank was going through, I was certainly enjoying each word because he was reminding me of my own past.

Meanwhile, he continued, "…it was Saturday, yes. I remember we were not supposed to go to college the next day and it all happened at the dinner table.

'So, don't you have a girlfriend?' Her mom asked, passing me the dishes. I coughed getting nervous.

Why do these people interfere in other people's lives? I thought and frowned.

'You are smart, how come you are single? You should be dating some hot girl,' she added.

'But Anamika is also beautiful. Does that mean she should also have a boyfriend?'

'Why are you dragging me into the matter? Please keep me out of it,' she said annoyed.

'Are you hiding something from us?' her mom asked.

'No, I don't have anybody,' she said.

Her mom went to the kitchen and I winked at her saying, 'Except me?'

She stroked my foot in reply and I blew her a flying kiss. We quietly had dinner and dispersed to our rooms without having any further conversation.

So am I smart… han? I was talking to myself. That day, for the first time, I missed my wife intensely. A random thought passed my mind making me shiver. It was about having Anamika beside me. A heap of thoughts overloaded my mind. Something deep down inside my heart made me feel alone. I wanted to change my situation, not for somebody else, but at least for my inner peace. And yes, I wanted Anamika. That night, I wanted her and not my wife. I couldn't sleep and went downstairs to the kitchen. I stayed there at least for half an hour, totally quiet, looking at her room. The light was switched on for she must have been studying. Her mom's room was dark. Nervousness took control over me and I began to make my way back.

"Promod," someone whispered and I jumped. I didn't know what happened as she took my wrist taking me towards her room. I got a little nervous, but I was safe in her room, which she locked. I began to sweat a little as she locked the door. Why did she do that?

'Why are you sweating?' she said caressing my cheek, making me shiver because it was the first time we had had any physical contact.

Was I at the right place or was I doing something wrong?

"Exactly at the right place," I shouted, making Mayank and Promod (the old man) jump in shock.

"You continue, uncle," Mayank said, showing me eyes full of rage.

…Yes, I was totally confused by the events of the evening. I was asking myself why was I there in her room. Interrupting my thoughts, Anamika again took my hand and made me sit on the bed. She kept her hands on my thighs, locking her fingers in mine. I was out of my mind, or was she? I was not able to make any guesses about what was going on.

'Look at me,' she said.

Damn! I was going to get crazy. I hadn't notice what she was wearing till then. Her cleavage exposed and her more than fair skinned breasts were trying to come out of her t-shirt. My eyes were beyond my control and got stuck there on her cleavage.

'What happened', she said casually, looking down at her own chest.

'Ohh, so this is making you sweat. Do you like them?'

I started inhaling deeply.

'You didn't like them?' She frowned and looked down.

'Oh my god! What's that?' she almost shouted in shock.

I looked down and was ashamed to have a huge bulge in my pajamas. Instantly keeping my hands over it, I said sorry.

Gathering herself, she asked shyly, 'Is it really that big?'

"Sir, chai," was the voice that interrupted us; we looked at the entrance of Promod's store.

"Yes, come in Bhola, but let me tell you, if they (I and Mayank) wouldn't have been here, then for sure I would have killed you for the timing of your entry."

Bhola went back smiling.

Promod continued.

…so let's come back. Yes, she was horrified to find the huge bulge.

It was the first time in my life I was looking at somebody's boobies, apart from my wife's.

'Tell me please?' She pleaded.

'What do you want to know?' I exclaimed.

'Aren't they nice?' she asked me and came closer. She took my hand and put it on her right breast. And I don't know what happened to me as I started squeezing it, making her moan. I rubbed my hands over her chest slowly and she squealed in pleasure. Suddenly, there was a knock on the door and someone called out her name. Shit. It was her mom!

I looked at Anamika, terrified. She, however, was cool as a cucumber. She straightened her t-shirt and led me to the window.

'Jump down and stay in the garden. I'll open the door as soon as mom goes to sleep,' she said planting a kiss on my lips.

I did as I was told and found a spot to lie down.

I woke up with someone shaking me. I thought it was a dream, but it was Anamika waking me up. The coast must have been clear.

Without wasting any time, I instantly gathered my senses and followed her into the house. As we entered, she went towards the kitchen and I went off to my room. The wall clock showed 4:35 a.m. I jumped on my bed and snuggled under the blanket and slept.

Shit! Something was inside my pajamas.

It was Anamika's hand holding my manhood. I opened my eyes. How did she get in?

'Hey, what are you doing here? Please go downstairs to your room. Now I don't want to sleep on the terrace,' I almost shouted at her.

"Shhhhh... don't shout, now she won't get up before eight as she took a sleeping pill," she said squeezing me hard. It was pure pleasure. We began kissing passionately and my hands seemed to have made their way to her chest on their own. She unhooked her bra and I began stroking her nipples that had become stiff. We caressed each other's tongues, mixing the saliva and gulping it, sucking the upper and the lower lips simultaneously. I threw the blanket off with my legs, taking her t-shirt off.

Was I in heaven or it certainly would have been a dream. I stumbled over the bed to see the most beautiful breasts. Without wasting a single second, I madly went over them, pushing her back over the pillow, making her moan loudly. As we were kissing passionately, I put my hand into her track pants. I entered her. She moaned and went extremely wild, taking my face in her hands and pulling me towards her. It was the first day and we did it thrice before her mother woke up.

We started sleeping together often after that. Then came a day when her mom caught us, and to our shock, she said nothing to us. And then came the most unbelievable day of my life. Get ready for a shock.

It was exam time. Anamika had gone to write hers while I was home preparing for mine. I and her mother chatted over breakfast and helped her clear the table. As I was washing the dishes, she suddenly came and hugged me tightly from behind. I didn't react, but asked her calmly, 'Is everything okay? Has something happened between you and uncle?'

"I want you Promod, you are very attractive."

"What does that mean?" My voice became loud.

She didn't say a word and coming towards me, closing her eyes, she put her lips on mine. I didn't react. As she was trying to get deep, I pushed her away.

'Please aunty, I hope you won't do this again. I love Anamika, and knowing it well, you are doing this with me!'

'But she will never get to know.'

'No means no. I can't betray her, not even in my dreams.'

'Okay, your wish,' she sounded glum.

I went upstairs and wasted my whole day, till Anamika came to my room in the evening.

She came smiling and hugged me.

"I love you Promod. Thank you for making mom believe that you really love me."

I felt I had been stabbed. How could she have told her?

I smiled and she gave me a nice thanks-giving session after that.

This went on till my last year there, as she was preparing for the IAS.

Time flew and life was going on smoothly for us. I planned to marry her without letting my parents know and get settled in Delhi. But all that was shattered by a letter that came just a few weeks before my last semester exams. The letter was from my father telling me about the bad health of my son. Anamika's mother read it, and I owe my life's happiness to her as she didn't disclose it to Anamika. But she warned me to leave and find myself another accommodation. She couldn't stand the betrayal.

For the first time, I saw her crying. She was a good lady, but I had betrayed both of them.

She asked me to pack my bags without letting Anamika know and even started sleeping with her so as to make sure that she wasn't able to come to me.

I shifted to Badarpur border for the last month and completed my engineering without trying to get in touch with Anamika.

Completing my degree, I came back to my town, and my son turned five the same month I returned. He started going to school. I had not even come once to see him. My father was very angry as I hadn't visited them even once in the last four years.

I was ashamed for my behaviour and my responsibility towards my family, and was also sad about Anamika. After coming back, I didn't touch my wife for almost two years. She became a machine, behaving like a lifeless creature who'd just work from morning till night.

I: So these were the bad deeds you committed?

Mayank: But except from the time you spent after coming back, the rest was awesome. I mean, you almost experienced heaven.

Old man: Only in those four years. But now I feel bad about how I betrayed my wife instead of feeling bad for Anamika. My wife is an awesome soul and I got to know this as we got closer.

I: OMG, it's dark outside and it's seven.

Old man: I guess we should leave now; dinner must be ready.

As he stood up, Mayank queried: Uncle, you didn't seem this tall while sitting.

"Son, I am 6'2."

Mayank: One foot taller than me.

We walked to Picture Palace where we found a white Toyota Fortuner waiting for us.

"Let's get in," Promod said and we got in.

We didn't talk much on the way and I was rather nervous about the narrow road we were speeding on. It was a drive of around two kilometres and it took almost fifteen minutes to reach a big black grilled gate. The driver honked and a guard came running to open the gate to reveal a huge mansion. Mayank pinched my thigh and I nodded with my mouth open and eyebrows raised.

"He's extremely rich, please behave properly," Mayank said getting down from the car.

"Uncle, what's that?" I said pointing towards a line of lights spread across a few hills.

"My son, that's the famous Woodstock School. It is a big place spread over all those hills. Unlike our Indian schools, it provides a high school diploma equivalent to a US high school diploma."

I made a mental note that I'd send my kids to this school.

"I think Tendulkar's son is studying in Woodstock," Mayank said.

"Come, let's sit inside," Promod started walking towards the entry of his mansion and both of us followed him.

His mansion was astounding. It really was decorated amazingly well. As we were busy praising its beauty, Promod interrupted us, "Please remember to keep mum about the secrets I have revealed." We nodded.

As we settled on one of the sofas, his wife came in.

"Let me introduce them," said Promod. "He's Gaurav and this is Mayank. They are from Delhi. They are pursuing engineering from my alma mater."

Mayank and I looked at each other as a reaction to the lie, but didn't say anything.

"Where is everybody?" he asked his wife.

Their son had gone to meet his in-laws with his wife and would return the next day. They had dropped off the children at Lal Tibba for shopping.

"Children?" I exclaimed.

"Yeah, our granddaughter has invited one of her friends for the vacation."

Promod called his granddaughter on the phone. She would be reaching home in five minutes. We waited for her.

Soon voices could be heard. I turned around and froze. My heart started pumping wildly. And the girl opposite me seemed to have the same reaction. Her jaw as well as the packet she was holding dropped. It was Shemona. And her friend Iyana.

Shemona was Promod's granddaughter. What luck! Mayank looked at me and smiled slyly.

We were soon gathered at the dining table. Promod introduced us and we quietly played along. As dinner began, Shemona rested her hand on my knee. Instantly, I pulled my leg back, hitting my chair with a loud thud.

"What happened?" Promod got nervous.

"Nothing, a mosquito bit me, I think."

Everyone laughed.

After dinner, we sat in the garden, having hot gulab jamuns for dessert.

My phone rang and it was my mother. I assured her of my well-being asking her not to get worried. As I was putting my phone back, the clock showed 8:53 p.m. I got a little worried.

I: I guess we should leave now.

Shemona interrupted before Promod could say anything.

Shemona: You can stay. Don't worry, the driver is here for the night and can drop you.

I: But it's already nine.

Promod: Yeah, they are right. It's too late.

We thanked all of them and I touched Promod's wife's feet and she blessed both of us. Mayank thanked them for the dinner as we were getting into the car.

I threw my hands in the air at Shemona, showing my phone as we had not even exchanged our numbers. She just smiled and waved.

The driver paced towards the Mall Road. It was dark and we were a little scared. Mayank asked the driver to slow down. He replied casually saying that he had grown up in those streets and wanted us to trust him blindly.

As we reached the Library's entrance the driver's phone rang.

"Yes sir, we are at the Library."

I don't know what Promod said, but the driver handed me his phone.

"Gaurav, it's me Promod. Listen, you guys pick up your bags from the hotel and stay here with us in our guest lodge."

I was rather surprised, but answered in the affirmative immediately. I felt a little guilty at having accepted the invitation too eagerly as I handed the phone back to the driver. Mayank was a little annoyed as well when I told him, but didn't say anything when I reminded him of the spooky hotel.

The driver parked the car. We entered the hotel and went up to the reception. There was a new person. We explained the situation to him.

"Yeah, he told me about you guys. You can take your bags, it's not an issue."

Mayank went to the room to get our bags while I waited and had a little chat with the man.

I: So, how many of you stay here at night?

Person at the reception: Four – one security guard, one chef and two caretakers, including me.

I: Don't you feel scared being alone in such a big building at night?

Person at the reception: No, it's been almost ten years now, we guys are used to it.

I: But, where are the other people?

Person at the reception: Two are out on field duty, marketing for us, and the chef is inside, cooking dinner.

Meanwhile, Mayank returned with the bags, putting them on the sofa.

I: Can I visit the kitchen to see what he's cooking tonight?

Person at the reception: Sure, it's this way.

He said pointing towards his right.

Mayank said: Come back fast, we have to go.

I nodded towards him.

I entered in a dimly-lit gallery but found nothing but a switchboard behind a curtain.

Person at the reception: Go to your right up the stairs.

I began making my way up the stairs. The walls were covered with faces of animals. There was a bend ahead. I was reluctant to go ahead and swallowed the lump in my throat. I went ahead only to find another bend. I walked slowly in the dim light, but froze as there was a face of a deer staring right at me. It was a painting. My heart skipped many a beat and I made a quick about turn. I ran back to the reception.

I reached the reception panting, only to find Mayank and the man in the midst of an argument.

Mayank: But the person sitting here in the afternoon asked us to pay nothing if we decided to leave tonight.

Person at the reception: But he didn't tell me anything, so you have to pay nine hundred bucks.

Mayank: Okay, call him. I'll make you talk to him.

Person at the reception: I don't have his number.

I mean, what exactly was he trying to do?

Interrupting Mayank, I said, "Okay then, we should leave now. Come on Mayank, I've got a call from Promod uncle."

Turning to the receptionist, I said, "Do you know Mr. Promod? He's our uncle and we are going to stay at his place. So thanks for keeping our bags safely.

The man looked shocked and nervous at the same time at the mention of Promod.

We finally left and the car zoomed towards Promod's place.

We found all four of them sitting in the garden exactly where we had left them. Promod came towards the car.

"Yay, our friends are back," Shemona shouted throwing her hands in the air.

Our bags were taken by the servant to the second floor of the guest house. According to Shemona, the view from that floor was amazing. I had a feeling that there was some other reason why she wanted us there.

After a chat with the family in the garden, it was time to retire. Shemona and Iyana escorted us to our room, showing us the view from the window.

"Don't sleep early, we are on the same floor connected by the balcony," she said.

So this was the reason behind us being put up on the second floor. I was on cloud nine. Everything was coming to me even before I asked for it. I must have done some good deeds.

Iyana winked at Mayank, but he didn't seem interested and just smiled at her.

"Let's sleep," Mayank stated.

"Are you serious?" I exclaimed. "And lose the wonderful opportunity of meeting a lovely girl at night? Dude, can't you guess why we are here on the second floor? It is connected to their room through the balcony."

"Yes, you are right; I didn't even think about it," Mayank finally said.

"Try your luck with Iyana; she isn't that bad and seems interested in you."

"No, let's sleep. We are their guests, and should maintain our dignity. We won't be able to go back home if somebody catches you doing anything like this. Don't you remember the terror in the eyes of the receptionist when we mentioned Promod?" said Mayank.

"Okay, you go to sleep but please don't spoil my night. Life gives you few choices, but it's you who has to decide what to choose and what not to." So instead of having no option but to choose what's left, scroll your options and choose what you think is the best for you.

"So I choose the booze," Mayank said bending on his knees, pointing his hands towards me, making them a handgun. Let's open our bottles. He unzipped the bag, handing me my small Magic Moment bottle and taking out his Antiquity bottle. He also pulled out a cold drink for me, as according to Mayank, mixing two liquids doesn't allow us to taste even one, so he prefered it neat (undiluted).

There was a small table with two chairs in the corner by the window where we sat. I was amazed with the view of the school down the valley as we switched off the lights. A soothing breeze came in as I opened the window. I was amazed, and closing my eyes, I let the slow sweet air kiss my face as my eyelashes danced with it. I wanted to stand there with my arms open till eternity, feeling the same love of god for me. Rocking my face upwards, eyes still closed, having one of the best feelings I ever had, it was my sister whom I missed at the moment. I wish she could have been there with me and we would've had the night-long talks sitting beside the window, looking into the valley.

We asked the house help for two glasses for our drinks. After having a few sips, I noticed a minor crack in my glass, so I called the man again and told him.

He said, "Okay, no problem."

"But you should see it, else you'd blame me for cracking it."

"Sir, it's totally fine," he said taking a few steps backwards as if we'd asked him to confess something and literally ran away.

We started laughing looking at each other.

"What the hell man, are we that scary?" Mayank said shockingly.

My phone rang. It was my sister calling, and I knew it was going to be a long call. Chatting away, I went into the lobby and before I knew it, I had reached the garden. I bumped into the helper and leaned towards him.

"What happened, sir?" he asked politely.

"Can't you see I am drunk?"

"Yes sir."

"Then what are you waiting for? Take me to my room."

He led me to my room and Mayank and I laughed loudly.

The loud laughter brought Shemona to our room. Her eyes opened wide as she saw us drinking. But she didn't say anything and instead gestured 'two' with her fingers before leaving. I wondered if she wanted two drinks or was asking me to wait till two.

It was midnight and both of us were talking in bed. Before long, Mayank began to snore. My thoughts wandered to Shemona as I stared at the clock on the wall. I wondered if she'd really turn up at two in the morning.

The next thing I remember was being jolted awake by someone pulling at my leg. It was Shemona.

Was she that desperate? It was time to find out.

I jumped out of the bed.

Shemona: So where should we go? Should we go to my room or the terrace?

I: Terrace! Are you sure? It'll be freezing at this hour.

Shemona: We can go to my room, but Iyana is still awake.

I: No problem, we can stay here…he's as good as dead.

Shemona: Are you sure?

I: More than anything.

I was certain about Mayank; and more than him, I was sure about his deep sleep after getting drunk.

I: So can we sit here on the bed?

I slipped under the blanket, pushing Mayank towards the end and asking Shemona to follow me and slip in beside me. She didn't take more than a second to do as I asked.

We looked at each other and without saying anything, I took her hand in mine. I grabbed her neck and pulled it towards me and started kissing her passionately. She moved herself accordingly and pulled me hard over her. I found myself over her and she looked stunning in the dim lighting of the room. Her face was glowing in the milky light, making me the happiest man in this world. The feeling I was going through was one of the best I had ever had. I looked into her eyes and she too was looking into mine. My hands made a move and were over her breasts. She moaned.

My hand went to her navel, to which she responded in a stroke shaking me as I was on her. I bit her lower lip. Getting my eyes a little away from hers, I looked at her in the dim glowing light, stopping every other move. Taking my right hand back from her breast and embracing her left cheek, and slowly scrolling my index finger from her eyebrow to her chin, I kissed her nose, forehead, ears, eyebrows and her eyes. I wanted them to be only mine for now. I was not able to take my eyes off her big beautiful eyes which were filled with the purest love. They were expecting, they was asking for my care, my trust and most importantly, my life. Continuously running my fingers through her hair, I licked her lips from left to right, and again and again, like a baby having his favourite ice-cream. She closed her eyes, bending her head a little backward with joy.

Grabbing my head, she pulled me closer and we both started kissing passionately. Our positions interchanged, she was automatically over me. My hands went under her t-shirt and pulled it upwards. I threw it away and started feeling the beauty of her body with my hands. I unhooked her bra and she started kissing my neck, pushing my chin up with her head. I threw her bra away as my hands fondled her breasts. She covered my hands and pressed them to massage her breasts. She kissed me on my ear and changing her position, she came beside me and slid her hand into my track pants.

"It's so hard!" she exclaimed.

"Yeah, and you are the reason."

She giggled and started shaking it. We both were without clothes within the next few minutes. I don't remember when we slept, but I woke up finding her in my arms like a baby kangaroo resting with its mom. Getting scared and shifting the blanket, I looked at the wall clock and was relieved to find that it was only four in the morning. I woke her up and she started searching for her clothes.

"I should leave," she said getting dressed.

"Sure," I replied pulling her towards me and kissing her again.

Mayank was talking in his sleep.

We both looked at him and laughed.

I guess he was the reason I had woken up.

Thank god, he saved us. She thanked him, to which I laughed.

It was the best night of my life till yet and will always be memorable.

She left and I slept, thanking Mayank for not waking up in the night.

Waking up at 8:30, Mayank kicked me, asking me to get ready. Without arguing, I went to the washroom and came back to answer Mayank's questions.

Mayank was surprised and questioned me about the seventeen-inch long strands of hair he found on the bed on my side. He counted them all.

I said, "I don't know anything about this."

"I know you must have invited some girl and had fun at night."

I realized he didn't remember any bit of our conversation of the previous night.

"Dude, it was you who was making faces at Iyana and giving her signals for the night. I fell asleep before you, so don't try to blame me for your deeds."

After my unbelievably confident lie confusing Mayank, I turned and started gathering our belongings.

Shemona knocked on the door and invited us to join them for breakfast.

Mayank headed towards the washroom and I took the chance to take Shemona's hand and pull her towards me. We started kissing. She enjoyed it for a few seconds and then took her hand away, leaving the room.

We felt a little embarrassed as everybody there was waiting for us when we reached the dining hall. We sat down.

I felt someone rubbing against my foot. It was Shemona again. I looked under the table and saw the foot coming towards me again. I pushed it a little hard and Iyana began to cough. I tried to figure it out, and yes, it was Iyana not Shemona who was patting me. It was Iyana who was rubbing my foot with hers! I felt a foot on my knee and looked up to see Shemona smiling. It was her this time. What a situation I was in.

After breakfast, we all sat in the garden and waited for the driver who was going to drop us to the stop from where we could take a cab to the famous Kempty Falls.

It was time to say our goodbyes. Promod wanted us to take his driver and car to the falls, but we politely declined. He had done so much for us already. We requested him to allow us to leave our bags in his showroom for the day and he readily said yes.

Taking our bags from the guest house, putting them into the car, we greeted everybody, touching Promod and his wife's feet to receive their blessings. I never leave an opportunity of getting a blessing from an elderly person. I believe it's the most valuable blessing a human can have.

In the car, I realized that I hadn't taken Shemona's contact number. But this time, I wanted to let it go. Let memories remain memories.

Leaving our bags at Promod's showroom, the driver dropped us at the Library Chowk and told us where we could get a shared taxi to Kempty Falls.

Reaching the taxi stand, we looked for private taxis, but they were charging an exorbitant rate. We went to the shared taxi stand and got a good deal. Two hundred bucks for the two of us is what we paid.

The taxi dropped us off at the stand near the falls. The driver said he'd give us three hours to roam about, but not more. We walked towards the falls and were greeted by a draught, and then by a mist of water. I stopped, closing my eyes and letting the water kiss my face. Taking two big boiled corns, we proceeded towards the cable car for the valley. We met a newly married couple in the cable car from Himachal. I was rather surprised that they had chosen this place for their honeymoon as they were from the hills, but I found out the reason. They boy's father didn't want them to go too far away, so they had settled for Mussoorie.

We reached the bottom of the valley and had some Maggi and cold drinks. We decided to go boating in the lake as well. There was a water ball at the Kempty Lake. I got into the water ball and the caretaker pushed it into the water. I was enjoying it at first, till I realized that there was a leakage and a little water was coming from that hole. I got scared and started screaming. Mayank laughed, unaware of my predicament. I was terrified and was sure I'd die very soon. As I screamed loudly,

Mayank finally realized something was amiss and asked the man to pull the ball out of the water. Drenched in sweat, I inhaled the pure oxygen relaxing my heart. Tears rolled down my eyes and I let out a sigh of relief. It was a real death bag! Thank goodness I was out of it unscathed.

We proceeded to the small stream near the fall which was deep into the valley. There was a dense forest that reminded us of horror movies. After taking a few pictures, we came back to the main falls, crossing it on the other side. We had lunch sitting at a restaurant from where the view of the falls was spectacular. People were splashing about in the water.

"Are you guys from Delhi?"

Turning around, we saw an extremely beautiful girl standing behind us.

"Yes, we are from Delhi. Do we guys know each other?" I asked.

"I am from Lajpat Nagar, you met me at Zook in Saket. Don't you remember?" she said pointing at Mayank.

I looked at him with my widened eyes.

"When did you go to Zook?" I asked Mayank.

"I don't remember," he replied with a puzzled expression.

Interrupting us, she held Mayank's hand saying, "Don't say you don't remember…how can you forget the night we spent together? Don't you remember that night you were totally drunk and you slept at my place?"

"What the hell is she saying?" I shouted at Mayank.

Mayank shrugged.

"How come she's saying things so confidently if you really don't know her?" I questioned as the girl seated herself on the empty chair at our table.

She turned and then screamed, "Come on, girls!"

We saw two more girls coming towards us.

I looked at Mayank questioningly, but he looked completely clueless. The two girls sat down as well and we exchanged fake smiles, having no other option.

They ordered a lot of stuff from the menu without talking much to us. We ignored them. Meanwhile, I was not getting positive vibes, so I kicked Mayank's foot and gestured at him to get up. We went to the billing counter. We were definitely not going to foot their bill!

Mayank went back to the girl. I don't know what exactly he was saying to her, but it seemed like he was convincing her about something. I saw them walking towards the cable car.

My phone rang and yes it was the call for which I was desperately waiting. It was my sister. I told her the situation we were in and she laughed declaring it a fact that I was always stuck with some girl at some point.

I tried to make it clear that it wasn't me but Mayank who had got stuck this time. After disconnecting the call, I turned around getting worried, as there was no sign of Mayank. To my relief, I saw him walking towards me in a few minutes.

As I began to question his disappearance, he only said that he didn't want to lose any more money and almost ran to get into the cable car.

He still looked worried, so I asked him what the matter was. Taking deep breaths he said,

"She trapped me. I really didn't know her, but she blackmailed me and almost shouted whether I was going to pay the bill or not. So instead of arguing and without asking for the bill, I just kept five hundred bucks on her table and came running to you."

I started laughing loudly, and after a minute, he began to smile. It was, after all, a rather funny situation.

We reached the taxi stand only to find that our taxi was gone. We had been cheated of a hundred bucks. Feeling helpless, we went into a nearby restaurant and asked the owner if he could help us get a taxi. I mentioned that we were Promod's guests, hoping that would help. The old man responded generously and asked us to sit and have a few snacks. He called one of his workers.

We sat down as instructed and ordered two cups of tea. Soon, the worker came back with a taxi driver who was willing to drop us at Library Chowk.

As we asked for bill, the owner told us that the snacks were complimentary for Promod Ji's guests. But I insisted and paid him.

After we reached Library Chowk, the taxi driver refused to take the fare, saying we were his guests, and India is well known for loving its guests. To make him take the fare, I told him that we'd tell Mr. Promod that the people of Mussoorie were not fair towards their earnings and don't even accept the normal wage that is needed to make a living, for the sake of being helpful and courteous towards their guests. He took it apologetically as he understood my words. I gave him a hundred bucks extra for his faithfulness towards his native place.

I checked my phone; it was 6:30 p.m. We had to rush to reach Picture Palace to take the last bus for Dehradun that left at 7:30 p.m. After a quick stop at a restaurant for a bite, we reached Promod's showroom. He was waiting for us. We told him everything we had gone through and how we took advantage of knowing him in this unknown city. We took our bags and Promod also accompanied us to the bus stand.

Reaching the bus stand, we thanked him profusely for making Mussoorie an experience rather than just a trip. Getting emotional, he stated something with all his inner sense which I didn't understand at that moment, but now whenever I see a child doing something for his living, I remember his words.

He said, "Pupils are considered as god and I wonder why god is left alone to strive for life, while on the other hand he is being bribed for prayers. I mean, why do people ignore the opportunity that they have in front of them rather than making an uncertain investment in places considered as god's home. I am not saying don't pray, I too pray, but to an unseen power that strengthens me. I sincerely believe in god, but for me, it's an unseen power that always stays with me.

"Whenever I want, I can sit alone and find my inner senses to make myself powerful. If it doesn't come out of praying to god, then I find children and help them in whatsoever way I can. You made me remember my college days and on the other hand you are of the age of my grandchildren, so I didn't help you, but instead showed my love and care for you by making you feel safe in an unknown city. I bet if you were of my age, we would have been a great trio. But I am sad that I don't have anybody like you whom I can share my feelings with.

"Enjoy the enrichment of your friendship, as I believe that you guys are really going to play a lifetime game of dealing with each other's unimaginable shit. What we call real friends are very few; if you find some, keep them, else regret would be the only option and loneliness will be the only partner. You were the ones who gave me a reason to miss my past, else I would have not even thought back on those times. You made me feel this happy that I don't have words to thank you guys. I wish you could stay longer. Have fun and let me know if you need any assistance in any city at whatever time. I'll try my best to fix things in your favor."

We touched his feet to show the respect we had for him, and he too blessed us with the best blessings he could have gathered, especially for our future. His driver, who was waiting for him, gave us the tickets with confirmed seats. Thanking him again, we boarded the bus, waving at him from the window. At this moment, I missed Shemona like a student missing an answer while writing an exam. I was not ready to accept the fact that we were really not meeting again, if not coincidentally.

The only way @Dehradun

$\divideontimes$

Missing her, I didn't realize the effect the chilly wind was having on my face. I didn't even notice that my nose was dripping. After we reached Dehradun, we went looking for a hotel. After walking for a couple of miles, we checked into Hotel Ashrey on Tyagi Road near the railway station. We were given room no. 314 on the third floor.

Ordering dinner in the room, we opened our bottles and made our drinks. After dinner, we got under the blankets and began chatting. Soon Mayank's phone rang. It was his girlfriend. I went out to the balcony. When I came back, I found him snoring loudly with his phone still stuck to his ear. And I could hear his girlfriend still talking. I picked up the phone, told her about the scenario and went to sleep.

Waking up early, Mayank had got to the bathroom first. I had a desperate urge to go to the loo. I screamed and told him to come out. He gave no heed, so I began banging on the door. He realized my urgency and came out. I rushed in and sat down on the pot. When you have to go, you just have to go.

After freshening up, we went down for breakfast. That was followed by a nap and a movie. We returned to our room and gathered our bags. We reached the bus stand and boarded the bus to Rishikesh. We even got seats together. It was 6.30 p.m. I asked a co-traveller how long it would take for us to get there. Two hours. I looked at Mayank and wondered if we'd be able to find a hotel that late. Mayank said we'd figure it out once we reached. He just wanted to sleep. Soon, the bus began moving. It picked up more passengers. It was packed in no time with people standing in the aisle.

"Will you please give this seat to me?" A voice said but I ignored it intentionally.

Yes, the female voice was asking *me* as this time I felt a tap on my shoulder. I turned around to find a lady of about thirty-five years of age. Instead of giving my seat to her, I thought about the two-hour journey ahead and how tired I was.

"Aunty, I would have given it to you, but I am a back patient and it hurts if I stand for too long. You're welcome to share the seat though. She refused and looked miffed.

She seemed fit and I was sure she wanted to take advantage of being a woman. But I was determined that I would not be taken advantage of.

Mayank was in deep sleep and was bent over the bag which he was holding in his arms. I was scared for him, for if the driver braked hard, he'd certainly hit the seat in front. I put my hand on his head as a precaution.

The driver did brake really hard, jolting everyone forward. Some of the passengers began shouting and abusing the driver, but everyone was safe. I too was safe and had also saved Mayank. But the impact had been so hard that my hand on Mayank's head hurt him.

He jumped up in pain and shouted, "Did someone ask you to put your hand here?"

"I'll kick your ass man, you'd have gotten hurt if I wouldn't have been here," I said annoyed.

"Let it be then, you should've left me to get hurt. Did I ask you for any kind of assistance?"

I got really mad and decided to ignore him. This time I tried to sleep, but I wasn't able to, so I decided to close my eyes and shut out the people of this cruel world.

The World of the Priests
@Rishikesh

✄

"Hey, we reached well in time. Let's hurry up and find a hotel," Mayank said pushing me. Asking an auto driver, we went to the government tourism office, hoping to get a room there. We were rather disappointed after speaking to the manager.

I: Can we have a room and what are its charges?

Manager: You can certainly have one, and the charges are two thousand rupees, exclusive of taxes.

I: But these are government tourism rooms, they should be cheaper?

Manager: Sir, we don't have any room cheaper than this. But if you want, I can take you to my friend's hotel. It's little far from here, but close to the Lakshman Jhula, which is in Tapovan. It is the most famous spot in Rishikesh.

Mayank: Okay, first call him and let us know if there are rooms available there, and the tariff also.

Manager: Yes, he does have vacant rooms. They usually charge fifteen hundred per room, but because of my reference, they would give you more than a fifty percent discount and would cost you seven hundred bucks per night.

I: Okay, take us there.

The manager brought around his bike. But there were three of us. Wouldn't that be a problem on a two wheeler?

"It's not a problem; the traffic police doesn't catch anyone." Not having any other choice, we had to trust him, so we sat adjusting ourselves. He accelerated the bike and I almost got a heart attack as my legs went up in the air and I grabbed the safety rod to save my butt from kissing the ground.

It was almost ten minutes since we started, and we were still on the road. Getting a little scared, I asked, "How far do we have to go?"

"We are going to the main tourist place in Rishikesh – Tapovan near the Lakshman Jhula, which is six kilometers away from the main city. It will take a few more minutes to reach there, as I don't want to speed.

"No no, don't speed, it's totally fine," I said analyzing the situation.

We finally reached Hotel Shivansh Inn. Mayank went to see the room as I filled up our details at the reception.

Mayank came down telling me that there was not even a single soul in the hotel.

"Don't you have any guests in the hotel?" I asked the person at the desk.

"Sir, we do have two rooms booked, and the rest of the rooms are booked for tomorrow, as we generally give our rooms to tour packages of more than twenty people."

"We can check-in," I said looking at Mayank and he nodded in approval.

Our room was on the first floor and had a big common balcony with the adjacent room, with two tables having cane chairs around them. It made me feel amazing and alive. It was dark and from the balcony I wasn't able to see anything but a mountain in the dim moonlight. Nothing was visible down the building as there were trees all around us. The best thing was the continuous sound of the gushing water of the river Ganga near the building.

It was one of the moments of joy in my life, and if I had been the owner of my life, then I certainly would have promised myself to stay in that room forever and write every evening sitting in the balcony. To satisfy my soul and live life generously, and to help people enjoy and give a meaning to their lives. With that thought, I rested my bum on the cane chair in the room. Mayank was flat on the bed and I was taken into some other world with the kind of thoughts going in my mind.

Mayank had started snoring and something in me forced me to go and sit in the balcony. The moment I stepped out of the room, something deep, really deep gave me a shiver. It seemed as if something inside me was forcing me to just stay and hear the consistent sound of the river. I was unable to move, so I grabbed the chair with a long step and sat there with one leg on the other, keeping my hands crossed. Closing my eyes, I rocked my head up and started inhaling the air deeply.

Everything I had ever enjoyed flashed through my mind, but there wasn't a single moment that gave me an inner feeling of happiness like the one I was going through.

Motionless I was, and the rustling sound of the leaves due to the zephyr mixed with the gushing of the flowing stream was making the pace of my heart slow. I wanted time to stop and freeze for a while. I was getting restless, so I went to the room and took out my diary and pen from my bag. Instead of switching on the balcony's light, I kept the room's door open and turned my table towards it. It was the first time that I had written a poem that fast.

Sitting on a cane chair with a paper and a pen,
Having a heap of feelings with the surroundings I have,

The stream is singing and the woods are playing,
Life's song with a wonder saying,

Leave the mundane things and come to me,
I'll show you the truth of an unknown glee,

Nature is speaking directly to me,
Not leaving me alone and making us 'we',

Closing my eyes I felt God closer,
And making a mark, he made me stronger,

The river is flowing continuously with a sweet noise,
Roaring like the power of a persistent voice,

Hearing the music of dancing leaves,
Can cheer up any heart, without anything to grieve,

It is the moment where I can find me,
Connecting with nature through the heart, and see,
Connecting with nature through the heart, and see...

I was satisfied with what I had penned down. Now, and closing the door, I sat in what seemed like never-ending joy.

"Have you seen that priest with long hair?"

This sentence broke my reverie and I turned around to see two girls.

"Oh, la la, we have neighbours now," one of them said clapping and jumping in a very innocent manner.

I smiled at them, and to my surprise, they came and sat next to me. I got to know that they were Japanese. I told them about the journey we'd completed and that we were there for two nights. They told me the reason behind their visit to India: they wanted to learn meditation, and according to them, the best place was India. We started cracking jokes and Mayank, who doesn't open an eye even after a series of kicks, came running. Power of a woman's laughter... half dead men also come alive.

He smiled at us as one of the girls said, "So he's your brother, right?"

"Yeah," I nodded. "They are our neighbors in this room," I said pointing to their room.

Interrupting, me she said, "We are going to make dinner as we've got a kitchen in our room. Do you guys want to join us?"

"No thanks!" I straightaway said, as they were strangers.

They went to their room and we went upstairs to the restaurant. We got back to find the girls sitting in the balcony. We went in without saying anything. Mayank took his bottle out, throwing mine to me. I took small sips, but Mayank had gone mad; he emptied half his bottle.

"Let me leave it for tomorrow," he said looking at his bottle. Closing the bottle tightly without saying anything to me, he slipped under the blanket and started snoring within a minute.

I laughed filling my glass again. As our room was lightened up by a dim light, I pulled the curtain aside to see if someone was sitting outside. And yes, one of those two Japanese girls was sitting alone. I went out wearing my hoodie.

I: Hey, you are still here?

She: Yeah, she was sleepy, but I wanted to enjoy the weather.

I: Do you…

Interrupting me she said: Are you having a drink?

I: Yeah, you want one?

She: I would love one if it's not a problem for you.

I: Oh, not at all, but the issue is that it's not cold.

She: I can ask for ice cubes from the room service.

Saying this, she went to her room and came back smiling.

She: He's coming with the ice cubes. Do you also want some?

I: Sure. That'll be nice, and it would help us empty this bottle.

The room service boy came smiling with a small bowl of ice cubes and she jumped clapping slowly, exactly like she had done when she found me there for the first time a few hours back. She looked really cute when she did that.

As the room service boy left, she grabbed the bottle, swiftly pouring the drink into the glass she brought from her room.

She: Do you want me to make a drink for you?

I: No, thank you, and I am not even someone who can drink it neat like you. I apologize for forgetting it, but I can't remember your name.

She: Manaka. And your name is Gaurav, right?

I nodded in approval and we both settled on the cane chairs bringing them a little closer.

I: So, do you like a place like this?

Manaka: The place is fine, but something is missing. Sitting at a place where one can feel nature so close. Everything is perfect: running water, the woods, a cottage, mountains, the moon, dim light, the wind and you.

I: You!

Manaka: Yeah you, we need someone to enjoy some memorable moments with. And you seem to be a good companion.

I: Really?

Manaka: Yes. You are calm, and seem to be understanding too. Most importantly, your eyes. When you smile, it makes me wonder what is hidden in them. You tell me or not, but I certainly know that there is something, something very deep. Something that is different from mediocrity. It's something big, huge or extraordinary. I doubt if it is love for someone, someone very special.

I was dazed and sat numb with the glass in my hand. I didn't have a single word to say. I wondered how she had learnt so much by just observing me.

I: I mean, what should I say? I really don't have any words.

Manaka: It isn't being observant, but your nature. Talking to you when we came made me feel like you talk about life. And when I first saw you with your hands crossed, chin up and eyes closed – you seemed mindful. I should tell you that I was thinking about you only before you came out. I don't know why, but I wanted to talk to you. I don't know why, but I wanted to spend time with you.

My mind stopped working; though I was not drunk yet, but her words were making me crazy. I didn't know if I was happy, sad, or shocked. I was dazed. Yes, I was. I just stared at her with the glass in my hand. She finally threw her hands in the air, asking me what had happened. I still didn't answer her.

Manaka: Gaurav!! Are you fine?

I: Yeah, (I said rocking my head swiftly both ways, like I had recovered from a shock.)

Manaka: Do you write? I noticed a diary on the table when we came in the evening.

I: Yeah, I do sometimes.

Manaka: I get it now, why I wanted to meet you. See, I told you that there is something deep. This is it.

She said, excited like a child.

I: Yeah, nothing can be deeper than this. So what exactly do you write about? And didn't you take advantage of this opportunity of having such an amazing place that gives 'our fingers the power to think like our mind'?

Manaka: 'Our fingers the power to think like our mind'. Nice thought. So you also play around with words…arranging them in such a manner that they make amazing sense!

I: Not really, but I think it's for the first time I did so, or maybe it's for the first time someone noticed.

Manaka: What exactly do you write? Thoughts like I do or are there some hidden talents?

I: Nothing much, but sometimes I write poems.

Without letting me speak, she interrupted.

Manaka: So you wrote a poem today, right? And if yes, then you are going to read it to me.

I: You want me to read it out now?

Manaka: I would love to hear it.

Without saying a word, I stood and went to the room. Coming back with my diary, I realized that she was making a very large drink. Maybe she wanted to enjoy the poem with large sips. I took my chair a little closer and our knees touched.

I: Are you ready?

Manaka: For you, always.

This time I sensed some other meaning in her words, but I began reciting the poem. As I finished reading out the last line, I felt her lips over mine. Leaving the diary in my lap, I opened my arms in surprise. This was the first time in my life that a girl was kissing me and I was not at all interested. She was getting intense, but I was just not interested. My 'saviour' rang and I took the opportunity to flee the scene with my diary in my hand. I ran into our room, locked the door and picked up my sister's call. After keeping the conversation as short as possible, I hung up and jumped into bed.

"Man, are you getting up? And if not, I'll go by myself."

Mayank was shouting at me. I woke up and asked him to give me twenty minutes to get ready.

As I came out of the room, I saw Mayank sitting with Manaka. I smiled at her, but she ignored me.

We went to the German café adjacent to the river Ganges and Lakshman Jhula for breakfast. Spending a few hours there, we found a place named 'Kamal Rest House' which was on the river bank and had a fantastic view. Its chef TC was famous among the Israelis and I must agree that his pancakes and papaya shake were delicious as well as healthy. We spent the entire day roaming around the town.

After dinner, we were sitting at the entrance to the Lakshman Jhula. It was around 8:30 p.m. and every shop there was closed. A person covered in a shawl was sitting there. He was asking every foreigner if they wanted any hash, weed or Bob Marley. Me and Mayank looked at each other and started laughing, asking him how could he be selling Bob Marley. Instead of replying, he smiled and continued his work. There came some man who said he was from Spain, sat with him taking a few drags from his cigarette. He confirmed the price and asked for some. And the one selling Bob Marley took a few minutes to bring the packet out from his hidden pocket. After the

Spanish customer left, he came to us and asked if we wanted anything. We shook our heads.

As we sat there, we heard voices.

"Is there a couple roaming around at this time?" I asked Mayank.

Soon we saw an Indian priest and a white lady.

"I won't take more than fifteen minutes, and I will not disappoint you", were the words of the priest.

I didn't know what he was trying to explain to the lady, but he sounded shady.

We both were sitting quietly and watching nature in its serenity. Suddenly we heard the voices of girls and saw a bunch of about fifteen girls heading towards us.

Mayank said, "Hey that girl is in our college's dental division and was from your school."

Though I didn't see her, but trusting Mayank I shouted, "Shilpaaa!"

Every girl that crossed us turned around. I was relieved to find that it was indeed Shilpa. She started walking towards me with a slow and unusual pace.

"Oh, it's you! I was wondering who knew me here," Shilpa said throwing her hands up in relief.

"What are you doing here and why are so many of you girls together?"

"We are here for a bachelorette's trip as one of us is getting married."

One of the girls called her from behind and she left.

We sat quietly again, and I was keenly looking at the monkeys swinging on the bridge, noticing how organized they were, without any rivalry between them. They were coming one by one to shake the wire. And when one approached the wire, the other would quietly go back.

Sitting there for almost thirty minutes, we realized that it was time to leave. Suddenly we heard some noise and saw the priest. The same one we had seen with the white woman.

As he came closer I tried to stop him and greeted him saying, "Radhe Radhe."

He said the same, but didn't stop.

"Where are you coming from?" I asked.

He finally stopped and said, "I went to drop a lady safely to her hotel."

"Yes, we saw you, but also heard a bit of your conversation with her. Don't get me wrong, but there seemed to be something between you two."

To our surprise, he sat down next to us and began to tell us his tale.

"She is my friend with benefits, or you can call her my girlfriend. She comes to India every year and has been doing that for the last five years.

"Are you serious?" Mayank almost shouted.

"What is the big deal? She wanted me and I satisfied her. And she continued coming every year to feel the essence of a holy place. Holy it really is!"

"Is there any holiness left after your deeds?" I asked.

"Don't you dare say another word, or I'll show you the power of being a priest."

"Don't get angry, man. I am sincerely proud of you and I said it sarcastically. I'd love to hear your tale," I said, just to calm him down.

He cleared his throat and started to speak.

Priest: It's been almost ten years since I've been searching for peace.

Mayank: Haven't you found it yet?

Priest: Not exactly. But yeah, I am getting closer.

I: You said you have been here since the last ten years, but you look quite young. What were you doing before that?

Priest: Not that young. I am forty-seven.

Mayank: Don't fool us, you are much younger.

Priest: Why would I lie? Regular yoga is the reason behind my youthful appearance.

I: What's your name?

Priest: Earlier I was Narender, but now I am Baba Narendra. Narender became Narendra and a normal human became a baba.

Mayank: So what exactly made you take this step into priesthood?

Baba Narendra: It was exactly what I wanted. You guys don't think I'm a person without wisdom. I am an engineer, a mechanical engineer.

Both of us looked at him in shock, with widened eyes.

Baba Narendra: I am not lying. I completed my engineering in 1987, and after working for a very reputed automobile company for fifteen years, I realized that I was doing nothing but wasting my time. But why are you guys so shocked by this fact?

Mayank: Both of us are also pursuing engineering, that too Mechanical Engineering.

Baba: Oh my god! Seems like I am sitting with my younger brothers.

He laughed wholeheartedly, with happiness coming from inside.

I: Didn't you get married?

Baba Narendra: Do you really think after getting married you would have found me here?

Mayank interrupted him.

Mayank: Don't you have a family? I mean, parents and siblings?

Baba Narendra: Yes, of course, I do.

I: Then don't you miss them?

Baba Narendra: Not at all. I don't even know how and where they are. This is the first thing that you have to leave when you go in search of something. You've to free yourself from all the things that you know will stop you, and according to me, family is the biggest setback which doesn't let you go even a single mile without letting the emotional ties pull you back.

I: But are you really free? I mean, the relation you have with that…

Getting my point, he reacted.

Baba: But I am not addicted to it. It was just for relieving each other.

Mayank: But it seemed like you were begging her, weren't you?

He looked at Mayank as if he was examining something closely.

Baba: Yeah, coz she cried as she was missing her family, and I wanted to relieve her from the pain. Haven't you heard the great saying, 'Sex relieves tension, but love causes it.' I was just making her feel alive, making her feel that she was not alone here.

I: So did you make her feel alive? She is beautiful.

Mayank: I agree.

Baba: You won't believe, but she's a mother of two and is forty-one. Few years back, she left her husband because of what she calls 'intimate partner violence'. Her husband used to take all her money and spend it on gambling. And sometimes he used to rape her brutally.

Mayank: Domestic violence? I thought the term belongs to our country only.

Baba: Not at all. I agree women are taken for granted in our country and violence is very common, but in spite of the respect they receive, there are instances there as well.

I: I don't understand why you aren't interested in knowing the whereabouts of your family.

Baba: Knowing the whereabouts of my family will fade the wisdom I have gained and will certainly force me to go back. If they're rich and happy, I'd want to join them to party. If they're poor and sad, I will get worried and will want to go and help them in some or the other way. So at least here, I am not bothered. What I am bothered about is to get closer to the truth, have peace of mind, disconnecting myself from everything happening in the world.

Mayank: Do you want to get some power and rule over the world?

Baba: No, but I want to let the world be and feel the presence of nobody. I just want the mind to rule over the body without disturbing even myself in the thought process. And if it happens, the world will know peace. No preachers would be required, everything will fall apart and people will experience the wisdom of living; they will get to know things they can't even imagine exist.

I: Do you want something to change, or you want it the way it is and get along with your own self? Would you like to share the experiences after getting to the point you want? I mean, will it be of any use to people like us?

Baba: No. What I have experienced till now would certainly be strange to you.

I: Strange?

I thought he was going to tell us something very profound, something rarely known and got curious about his next word.

Baba: Yeah, I am going to tell you the nature that surrounds us (priests). We people become egoistic and short tempered. I still don't know the reason behind it, but maybe because of the level of knowledge we gain. I am talking with you guys normally at this moment, but if you'd come at the time of my practice, then certainly I won't like it and without any reason I'll lose my temper.

I: It's fine, but you didn't tell us the reason for not sharing the knowledge you have?

Baba: Yeah, I wanted to make it clear that what normal people call sharing – somebody comes to them and gives them something without even asking for it. So knowledge too is an experience that you want a person to come and give you by keeping your body and mind at rest. Don't mind, but the truth is that nothing in this world is free. You go to school and you pay, you go to some different classes and you pay, anything you want is something you pay for. And yes, you even payback to your parents. Nothing in this world is free. Then why do you people want us to share the experiences that we've gone through, without going through anything yourselves. We don't charge people, but our biggest and the only fee is you walking down to us. At least one should have an urge to know something, only then we'll be able to make him understand. Our knowledge is not something that we can share by going to just anyone we want. A person should have a deep sense of thinking or feeling things, only then he'd be able to at least imagine what we've gone through. So the main thing I'm trying to tell you is that our practice itself makes us tired and we want to get away from the world. So if a person will approach us, we certainly will let him know the details till the extent he wants. But we won't approach anyone for sharing the knowledge we have, because it's something we get after days and nights of hardship. I had stayed under the sky an entire rainy night trying to get closer to God, trying to find my moment of peace.

Mayank: Did you find it that night?

Baba: Not exactly, but that night made me realize a truth of our beliefs and the mind set towards the work we are doing.

I: Can you please keep the explanation simple so that we can understand.

Baba: Yeah. I wanted to tell you something about the power of our beliefs. Not those beliefs that are given or imposed by some other being, but the beliefs that are made by our own mind. And the most important thing is that beliefs are not something that are made without any reason. They are made by our mind through the continuous approach of the heart. But, the most important question about the beliefs is that where do they arise from? What exactly generates a thought this strong that it becomes a belief?

The very common and widely known answer for this is the 'need' of a man, according to his living or thinking standards, that makes a person feel uneasy, and thinking further makes it a key thought to fulfil. And after it becomes a key thought, it is widely needed by a person's heart. Then there comes a saturation point between these thoughts according to the person's wisdom power and thinking process. If a person is a normal human being, without any high expectations, then he leaves the thought and keeps moving with his normal pace of life. But if the person is an extraordinary one, having great thoughts even with a little enthusiasm, then the game begins and the thought becomes a belief, and his aspiration becomes stronger towards achieving it. As a thought becomes a belief, it changes everything around. It makes you feel alive and away from mediocrity. A normal person will be way more productive than he'd ever been. His thinking will automatically change and every move will have a spark of new opportunities. Getting closer to his beliefs, he gets stronger for every next move. And, as he starts loving his moves, he gains the power over his own heart, providing the right direction to every move, achieving every goal and preparing for some bigger ones. Again, there comes something in his belief list for which he fights again and certainly wins the game.

I: Agree with your point, but one thing that I should ask you is about the payback part. As you said, a person has to pay back to the parents.

Baba: You got me right, but on the wrong part. I didn't mean it in the way you think. Listen carefully; you must have heard of the relationship between the old man who planted a mango tree and was asked if he'd be able to take advantage of its ripe fruits. He beautifully answered, 'I am not planting it for myself, but for my next generations'. He wanted the tree to help or payback his next generations, but he didn't want it to get wasted. They are being selfless.

This is something similar in the nature of parents. They don't want their children to payback; they just expect, rather trust them to make their old age painless and happy.

Let me try to explain it with a small example:

They do everything for us since our childhood. I mean, every need of a child is totally dependent on the guardian. They too never step back from their responsibilities of making the child happy. Sometimes they even stretch their limits to fulfill the requirements of the child. This moment, I am not talking about the rich people, but I am speaking for the masses who aren't rich enough to spend money without thinking. A time comes when the child is going to complete his studies, then we generally hear statements that only then will the parents be relieved. As if they were waiting for this time to come. And if they really were, this shows that the main reason was getting free from their responsibilities. The responsibilities were never a burden, but the child was a lifetime investment for which they were waiting to get a payback.

Silence! And I could feel the wind flowing through my hair. We remained still.

Baba: Are both of you still with me?

Mayank: Yeah, we are. Can I ask you one thing? How long did it take to grow your long beard? I'd love to have one.

Baba: It took ten years.

They both chuckled, but I was still busy framing my next question.

I: You told us about parents being expectant. But you didn't explain the fact of calling them selfless, at least for their children. I agree with your view with the examples you provided. Not only in our society, but across the world parents are considered selfless by their children. Why is that, and can you justify it as wrong, as according to you they too want a payback.

I thought I would make him nervous, but instead, he laughed with ease, looking at the sky, taking a deep breath.

Baba: I think I've got someone really sincere about the subject of life. I like the way you ask questions. I should thank you for questioning me. I never got an opportunity to guide someone in such a beautiful manner.

Interrupting him.

I: I hope my query isn't annoying to you?

Baba: Come on, my son! Rather I should say you are making me happy by asking questions whose answers you must be looking for. Let me try to explain the theory of parents being selfless in the best way.

First off all, I request you to not get my words wrong as I didn't say that they are not selfless, but I just said that they want a payback. And I apologize for forgetting the fact that I am sitting with engineers, that too mechanical engineers. Dealing with normal people is not a problem, but having someone from the same breed and a deep thinker at that is certainly a reason to play safe with words. It certainly is a truth that parents are selfless, but the reasons behind this are totally different from the ones we perceive. The first reason behind being selfless towards one's child is not the child's innocence, but the decision of the parents to force a soul to come into this world. He didn't come on his own, but because of the need or wish of the parents. And, as the child is small, innocent and helpless, then it becomes their duty to nurture the one they've decided to bring into their lives. They are selfless because they want the child to totally rely upon them and trust them, so that he would never be lost in the world. The duty of the parents is not just packing their bags for school, but a lot more – from providing the wisdom of 'why we breathe' to the level of patiently dying. They don't ask for anything, but just want them to know their responsibility towards their parents. They are selfless at giving, but they want them to understand and feel the fragrance of the essence of bounded love.

One very important reason behind this, which can't be negotiated, is that the blood that flows in the child's veins came from the parents, and I am sure that you wouldn't ever let go of even a drop of your blood. The last but not the least are the dreams that the parents embraced at the time of planning to have a baby, and they never want the dream to shatter. So it becomes their belief that the good upbringing of the child is mandatory for making him deal with this Jovian world. They forget everything else getting immersed in the selfless care of the one.

I: So you want to complicate it? They are selfish and selfless at the same time?

Interrupting me Baba said,

Baba: No, it's not being selfish. Okay, let me make it easier, as misinterpreting parents would not be a good thing. They don't want anything, but just rewards in form of their children achieving great heights. Their happiness is totally proportional to the kind of growth their children achieve in whichever respective fields they are. Parents never bind their children, but just wish to have them around during their bad times. Now it depends on you if you'd like to call it a payback, a ritual or a responsibility.

I: And what about people whose children don't obey them at all?

Baba: A pure state where we are certain about their lack of blessings.

Mayank: Lack of blessings?

I: Yeah, he wants us to understand that blessings work and don't waste even a single one when you have an opportunity.

Baba: Am I sitting with some preacher?

I hesitated, but didn't react. Instead I asked for his views by making a gesture using my hand and rocking my head.

Baba: He's right. But I should tell you a few more aspects, so you won't fall for the wrong ones…because a blessing is only counted as a blessing when it's given from a free heart and not from the one with selfish deeds. And, the purest blessings are again from parents. Don't blame me for coming back to them again and again, but this universal truth can never be challenged. I am not asking you to go and ask for blessings from your parents, but rather do just one thing and your day would be filled with some different kind of energy, which even you won't understand.

I: What's that one thing?

Baba: I got to know that you know a lot of things, and if not, you are searching for them. I am sitting here only because of your quest for truth. He isn't speaking much (Baba said pointing towards Mayank), and I am sure that he too knows a lot, but he isn't looking or searching for something like you. I request you to continue seeking your answers.

Mayank: Please tell us that one thing?

I looked at Mayank.

Baba: So let me tell you that one mantra of making your lives easy and smooth, as this is something equivalent to all other blessings in this world. You don't have to ask for anything, but touch your parents' feet every morning or whatever time you see them first in the day, to grasp all the positive energy they have. It isn't like you have to force them to say something over this step of yours, but you just have to make it a ritual, being the most important move in a day. Bending down every day to touch your parents' feet may not seem like a good idea right now. But I assure you, you should force yourself for a week and then you won't even notice how smoothly it goes, starting your day with the most powerful of blessings.

Rather, I would love to spread this knowledge and ask people to make it a ritual from their heart and not just for achieving some goals. And, why do I say parents? Because they are the only ones who'd never settle for less if it comes to their children and would love to give away everything for them. They've the purest blessings in this whole world as they don't have anything bigger than the growth of their children. So they don't compromise, at least not in giving away the blessings. As it's said, nothing in this world is bigger than the shelter of parents' love. There is also a well-known saying:

'I can't reach the skies' heights today, that's why I am touching my parents' feet; don't get worried, I'll bounce back very soon.'

Now, I should tell you the second person whose blessings will definitely make a difference. With due respect, it is our teachers, who – after our parents – are the only ones trying to make things better for us. I remember, even the Great Alexander said, 'I am indebted to my father for living, but to my teacher for living well.'

Yes, for you (he said looking towards me), please don't misinterpret my words as I didn't ask you to touch your teachers' feet. Though you can do it occasionally, but if you want to make it regular, then it's your choice. But I just request you to respect your teachers from the heart, so you can comprehend exactly what they are working out for you, and you too can apply your energy in the same direction.

Silence! And again I felt the prophetic wind.

Baba: If you remember, we were talking about payback, and I made it clear that our payback is a person approaching us. Let me tell you about the payback of the teachers apart from the fee you pay and the salary they get. The salary part is not the only reason for giving away life-making knowledge they have gained over the years, but the feeling of saying, 'This is a student I taught', say after twenty years when you'll get to some heights. It's a feeling of pride, incomparable to anything else. The only payback they want is to be respected by their students and nothing else. They also feel proud like our parents in making us a 'human of notice'.

Interrupting him,

I: Yes, I agree. I remember the words of my physics teacher Mrs. Arpana Handa, when I was in school. She said it was really bad seeing past students doing nothing but gossiping at bus stops as it felt like their hard work had been in vain. I clearly remember that she almost had tears in her eyes just at the thought of her students not doing well.

Mayank: I've also noticed the giving nature of teachers. Don't you remember (Mayank said nodding towards me), whenever we approached Mr. K.K. Gupta, he'd never refuse to make things clear, no matter how busy he was. I also noticed the behaviour of mature teachers, which is totally opposite of a normal human being, as they never have any mean words even for students like us who make them mad almost every time they take a class. He was a teacher I should thank profusely. After all, he inspired us to complete our first year backlogs. He was always patient, and sometimes we felt like he hated us. Do you remember the time we thought of going to him and I was sure he wouldn't help us? But you insisted and he seemed happy to help us. In spite of approaching him a lot of times, he never refused. He's our Power Plant teacher (Mayank made it clear to Baba).

Baba: See! All of us know it, but to understand, we need a kick of heavy emotions, and a place like this.

All three of us laughed.

Baba: You guys know all the things very well, but don't take advantage and feel proud because you were busy being the one you aren't. Yes, you pretend, unlike me. You guys have fake personalities.

You guys look perfect, but the fakeness behind these faces is not the only thing needed to live in this world. I am not asking you to throw away the facade and be who you are, because I know the circumstances that you live through every single day. I too lived in the same world at one time. And once you start working, you'll meet fake people and this quality will help you judge them.

Silence!

Mayank: So according to you, parents and teachers are the two main sources of the purest blessings?

Baba: Let me first complete what I was saying. Did I conclude?

I almost laughed at Mayank being sarcastically dumbed by Baba Narendra.

Baba: Apart from these two, we have another two sets of people – the first one consists of aged men. Old people have lived their lives and want people to do or achieve something in the one life they've got. As these people have almost reached the end of their lives and have felt the lack of blessings, they don't want anyone else to feel the same. So they are generous with their blessings. According to the elderly people, a blessing is not a cheat code or something, but the only part which is above hard work and proper planning. A wise man said, 'Blessings work even when you aren't working'. I got to know this long back, when I was your age. I started smiling, wishing and touching the feet of every old being I met anywhere. And it worked. I got the things I was searching for and the blessings worked for every task I undertook. I also realized that things aren't as tough as they seem to be. And, all of this I realized only after I got the knowledge I am giving you. I continued doing so and it became my ritual to respect the people I've mentioned.

I: Hmm. You mentioned two different beings, but you named only one. Who's the other one?

Baba: You guys are going to laugh when I tell you this category of people. Yes, they are random people, almost everybody whom we don't know personally. According to human nature, we are happy or unaffected with a person's growth if we don't know him; but if we know him, there starts a sort of rivalry, though not physically, but inside the cruel mind.

I request you not to misinterpret me this time as I've mentioned known people. For example, let's talk about you guys. I can tell you that you two will always lend your extra support if needed. So let's come to the general point we were talking about. We can be blessed by every other person walking down the street, but generally nobody wastes their words as they are not going to get anything in return. So a blessing from anyone without having hard feelings is a blessing to be noted in your account, depending on the purity of the person's heart towards you.

Silence! But Narendra took deep breaths closing his eyes and rocking his head in clockwise direction making a circle, twice.

Baba: Now, I would like to conclude, making you guys happy, as I'm certain you were waiting for this moment. So the secret behind a person's success or failure is his own attitude towards it and not any other thing. He can get everything he wants, just by following a few rituals that will make him pure and preferable. Let's talk about blessings; the most important part. I've told you that the biggest fount of blessings are parents.

Silence again, but this time Narendra seemed to have gotten lost in his thoughts. When he spoke, a gloom seemed to have come over his face.

Baba: Let me try to make it easier by putting them in points for you guys.

Parents: The biggest source of the purest blessings that ever exist. The best possible way to get them is to touch their feet every morning, to inherit the unseen power that resides in them. It can also be called a Midas touch that you can perform to nurture yourself. And if you can't do anything else, then just try to at least wish them 'good morning' with the purest emotions you have. Just respect them, as this is the only thing they seek from their children.

Teachers: The second biggest source of making your lives easier. They work on shaping your future and also analyze things on your behalf to show you the right direction, instead of wasting your time elsewhere. They also need one thing in return and that again is the same – respect. True respect comes from your heart and not just by faking it externally. Respect them as they bring out the best in you. Respecting your teacher makes you respect every aspect of your future, and future is something we live for.

Elderly people: The third biggest source of blessings across the world. Sometimes their intensity is so high that their blessings are more powerful than the first two, depending upon the nature of respect that you make them feel. If you are good to them, then they don't want to settle for any less, rather they would give all of the heart's purest blessings. You won't believe but pure blessings can perform miracles.

Unknown people: Any common man walking down the street can bless you to some extent. They want just one thing as well – respect. A smile makes them feel that yes, you care in some or the other way, and the people would give you the best blessings they have. A smile, a gesture and an expression are the ways to let someone know that humanity is alive. Blessings will be exchanged. And, who knows, you may get the bigger share.

I don't know why, but yes, I interrupted Baba.

I: Instead of doing anything else, we should strive to respect everyone in the family, our friends and even strangers then, I guess.

I thought he'd get angry, but Baba contradicted me.

Baba: Now I can say that I am certainly sitting with engineers. But I wonder why they are just sitting here and are unknown to people around for the beauty of thoughts they have. I was just checking by telling you the really common good things I knew, that almost everybody knows, but nobody applies. But you guys are surprising me with the hidden knowledge you have. I don't know what you are seeking, but yes, it certainly is something even I can't guess. It may be truth, but not peace.

I: That is something even I don't know, but yes, there is something I want to know, but what exactly it is, is still a question for me.

Baba: So can we try to find out?

Mayank: Yeah, carry on. Even I want to know what he's up to.

I nodded at Baba in approval.

Baba: Tell me just one thing that you like to do the most.

I: There are many and not just one.

Baba: Okay, let me ask it another way. Tell me one thing that you want to have, or what is that something which you can imagine in front of you that you long for.

I: Now I got you. It isn't something much, but just a cottage in some hill station like Mussoorie where I can live for a few months every year.

Baba: But where do you want to spend the rest of the months, which you aren't going to spend in your cottage?

I: I just want to travel to different places around the world, but come back to my cottage after that.

Baba: So I should tell you what I can get through your words. It's not fame that you are after, but inner peace, and you want to travel alone to different places around the world making friends who can visit you when you are home. I wonder why you want to travel alone, though. I guess you don't have anyone in your life, I mean a girlfriend, right? Okay, leave it. And another thing that I can see is your love for your country, as you said you wanted to travel around the world, but you want to come back and rest at home.

I: If the ball would have been in my court, then I'd quote, 'If travelling was free, you'd never see me again'.

Baba laughed out loud, rocking his head upwards, clapping.

Mayank: Baba, most of the times, I think I hurt people as I am straightforward and people get offended.

Baba: You have to become apologetic.

Mayank: Why apologetic?

Baba: Okay, let me tell you one thing that's as important as the blessings part. You said you offend people, right? But have you ever thought what impact it has on you. Maybe a few of them curse you at times, and I should tell you that a curse can nullify a blessing when it comes from a pure heart. So I just request you both not to hurt anybody to the extent that would force them to curse you.

I: Sometimes it becomes very difficult to ignore a person who is continuously shouting at you or annoying you.

Baba: I agree. But the only thing you need to do is to keep quiet instead of reacting. Don't react, but just respond with a smile; and if you can't even smile, then just make yourself strong enough so you can keep peace with yourself at least in that moment.

Mayank: But what if somebody is abusing you?

Baba: That is the most important situation when you need to keep yourself calm. I have tweaked George Bernard Shaw's quote for a situation like this:

'Not to wrestle with a pig, because first it'll take you to its level and then beat you with experience, besides enjoying it.'

So just keep on watching and listening instead of reacting in a manner that'd affect you in some way, because sitting quietly will result in miracles and the opposite will end up in a wrestle. I hope you are getting me.

Mayank and I looked at each other and nodded looking at Baba.

Baba: It would also help you lead a peaceful life without having rivals. And, a life spent without rivals is a life spent in God's conscience. If you are spending it in god's conscience, then imagination is merely a very small word to describe what miracles a human body getting instructions from the mind can perform.

I: Can you explain what love is?

Baba: Wow man! Do you really want to go so deep? You are getting intense, and that too in the most serious way.

I: But I really want to know, and I am also ready to spend the night here with you, and if you want, we can go to our hotel.

Baba: I would have answered you, but I have a person much more experienced than me to answer this question. And at this hour, we can also easily find her, as she must be inside her sleeping bag.

I: Her?

Baba: Can't a woman become a priest? (He said in an angry tone)

I: I didn't mean that, but I was asking how a woman can be reachable at this time and why would she speak with us?

Baba: She knows me very well and I'll introduce you guys to her by letting her know your quest.

I: Should we go?

Baba: Sure.

Looking at his phone's screen, Mayank said hesitantly,

Mayank: Dude, it is past midnight, we can continue tomorrow.

I realized Mayank didn't want to go at all. But I also didn't want to lose the opportunity of meeting someone who could open my mind to such an extent. I just made a gesture with my hand towards the other side of the river, where Baba was taking us. Having no other option, Mayank followed us. In the middle of the bridge, I got a shiver that shook my whole body. But the other two did not notice as Mayank and Baba were talking and walking ahead. It seemed like I had a cramp in my right calf, so I had to hold the bridges' fencing. I almost sat like a monkey, getting scared by the roar of the Ganges. An extremely cold wind hit me and I stood up in seconds. After walking a few steps, I looked back at the spot and sensed a fear equivalent to the fear of a deer when chased by a lion. Suddenly I realized that my cramp had disappeared. Was it something to scare me or was it some miracle to make me aware of the unseen power residing at that place? I reached them as they turned right after crossing the river.

Mayank looked worried and Baba was reassuring him.

"You guys please don't worry, in this place nobody will harm you and people will only help you in whatever way they can. God resides here."

'God resides here', are the words that took me back to the instance when I had sat down on the bridge a few minutes ago. Was it God who gave me the cramp, or was it the devil whose cramp was fixed by God within seconds, just to make sure of the wellbeing of a person in the place He resides.

Baba pointed to a corner under a tin shed in front of a shop. It seemed like someone was sleeping there. It was Jyoti, he said. I could see her in a blue sleeping bag, changing her sleeping positions. We could see her only because of the street light beside the tin shed. Without calling her name, Baba started giving us instructions about her nature and the beautiful life she was leading as one of the most respected and selfless priests of the area.

She must have been awake, for after a moment, the sleeping bag opened and her head popped out.

"Oh... It's you Narendra," she said with a broad smile on her face.

She didn't stand, but kept sitting in her bag.

She wasn't young, but seemed to be the same age as Narendra.

Baba: See, these are two extremely sincere engineers, but are philosophy students as well. I befriended the two about three hours back, but now I feel like I've know them for years. This guy (Baba said pointing towards me) wants to go deep into the heart and know what love is. So without any hesitation, I brought them to you as you could explain it better.

I was standing looking at Jyoti, just to see her reaction.

Jyoti: That's so nice of you. And now I got to know why I wasn't able to sleep; it just was because my day wasn't complete as I had to share my piece of being with these beautiful toddler souls.

She replied elegantly, as if she was an expert in the field of love.

Mayank interrupted, "Are you an expert in the field of love? I mean why did he bring us only to you and not to someone else?"

Jyoti laughed loudly, rocking her head upwards.

Jyoti said, "It is the respect they give me. Since he feels I can clarify and make you aware of what you want to know, I am pretty sure that I won't let him down."

"So finally, tonight, I'll sleep with the dreams of wisdom."

Saying this, I looked towards the sky, taking a long and deep breath closing my eyes with an incomparable sense of calmness.

"Probably you won't get to sleep tonight," Jyoti said.

Her words made me jerk my head towards her from the sky. She had the most sincere smile on her face. I had to gulp the truth that she was really going to keep us for a long time. But on the other hand I was happy about the fact that I was going to sleep with a different state of mind and probably with an inner peace. I realized that no one was taking the conversation along, so I tried.

I: Is our conversation going to end before the fowl's morning alarm?

Baba: We don't have fowls here. But yes, your wish would be considered by the chirruping birds.

Baba looked at Jyoti and gestured that he wanted to leave. But, to my surprise, she didn't allow him to leave, maybe because she wasn't comfortable with me and Mayank alone or maybe she wanted him to listen to the tale of love.

Getting irritated, Mayank interrupted, "So can you please tell us what love is?"

I never thought he'd be rude to a much respected stranger, and a lady at that. I wanted to shout at him, but before I could say anything, a voice interrupted my thoughts.

Jyoti: Whatever it is, but this is not love.

I was trying to understand her words. Was she trying to clarify something about love or was she trying to snub Mayank with her words..

Jyoti: Do not think I am making you feel low. But it was an instant answer to your rudely beautiful question.

Mayank: I am really sorry, but I didn't mean this. I mean, I wasn't trying to make you feel bad, but maybe because of the lack of sleep, I sounded harsh.

Jyoti: Hmmm, I can see that. If you want, you can leave us and get some sleep. According to Baba, you aren't as eager to learn as your friend is.

I: No, it isn't like that, but maybe because he's quiet, he appears uninterested.

Jyoti stared at me through the corner of her eyes and I felt bad for having contradicted her.

Mayank: No, its fine. I'll stay up.

Interrupting the conversation, I began with my doubt;

I: So what exactly is this thing or feeling or nature that we refer to as love.

As I was still figuring out what I'd asked, Jyoti distracted my thought.

Jyoti: It's nothing but the exact feelings that you have right now. Love to know what love is. I mean, it really sounds great. The urge to get something, the kind of feeling your mother must have had when you left for the trip, and the feeling to sit or roam around the woods and see mountains that one of you must be having.

I: Yeah, but how deep can it go and what changes can it make?

Jyoti: I request you to have peace with knowledge. Don't show the urge now, we aren't in any hurry. Are you?

Mayank: Not at all.

Silence! I wanted to interrupt, but didn't, as she seemed to be thinking of how to explain herself better to us.

Jyoti: If we talk about truly being in love with somebody or something, then you can see me or Narendra or many other people who've left their homes just to overcome the feeling of love for their desires. I'll try to give you an understandable example with a deeper hidden pain of love. It's the love of that father who gives money to his spoilt son every time. He never wants to lose his son and wants him to get better. In a case like this, he dies of that pain every day, without even being noticed by anyone. The limits of his pain are unimaginable and of the love, not even understandable, as his love starts when he is in the deepest of pain. Do any of you like the mountains?

I: Yeah, I do.

Jyoti: Don't you? (She said looking at Mayank)

I: He only likes it when people are dancing around.

All of us laughed.

Jyoti: So, have you been to a religious place?

I: Yeah I've been to Gangotri, trekking up to Gomukh where the River Ganges starts.

Baba: That's amazing. Seems like you are a religious person.

I: Not exactly, but I like visiting places that are less crowded and give us real time to be with ourselves. As introspection is one of the most important things in life and crowded cities don't give you that ambience to do so.

Jyoti: So you've been to Gomukh, which means you've felt the love for life with a heart closer to God.

I: I didn't find anything like that there, but it really made me feel like there can't be a better place to spend time with oneself. I remember, when I was walking in the clouds climbing up to Gomukh, I found water coming out from a cave-like structure. Those huge mountains which looked like a cave were made of ice. Ice, not snow. It was an experience that I can't explain in words. An experience of a lifetime perhaps.

Baba: Was there a moment when you felt alone?

I: There was a moment when I felt closer to god. You may call it closer to the end, or closer to life, or even closer to know what exactly everything means. But coming back to Delhi, everything vanished and life went back to its normal routine. But I had become aware of the truth, which I summed up in words: 'nothing is everything and everything is nothing.'

Jyoti: How do you think you got it? Do you have any idea what it takes to get exactly what you had? I should tell you what you had given to have those feelings: You travelled around five hundred kilometres to reach there, after which you trekked for almost twenty more. And above all, you had an urge with the purest feelings to get there. This urge or feeling to have or achieve something is what we call 'love'.

Mayank: You mean to say that the desire to have or achieve something is referred to as love?

Jyoti: No! You got me wrong. Understand my words clearly, without manipulating them in your own way. I said, 'what you give away in terms of passion or urge or the strong and never-ending feeling with enthusiasm to satisfy yourself in every possible manner is love'.

Sometimes love is being trapped by greed as well. As I gave you the example of the loving father – his love was pure and most intense, but he was doing it for the greed of keeping his son with him. Love is the most beautiful feeling, but sometimes we find it in the strangest places and in the most inappropriate manner.

I: Do you have an example of it being in the strangest place?

Jyoti: Yeah sure, I do. Have you seen a poor person who is an alcoholic and trapped in the habit of drinking?

I: Yes.

Jyoti: Then you must have also heard tales of the extent he'd go to, to get money for a bottle, and very often you hear in the news that a person has killed his mother, wife of any other member of his family just because they were not giving him the money to buy a drink. The mind of a person like this is distorted to an extent that he even takes the life of another human just to fulfill his wish. I don't think there can be a bigger example of being in love with something, though I truly agree that it's completely wrong, but he commits the sin just to get closer to his addiction. Love can exist in the most bizarre of situations. So, apply wisdom to your thought before executing it.

Baba: Don't you think we are taking this in a wrong direction. I mean, you are giving eminent prodigious examples, but still we are not helping these wonderful souls get closer to what they are looking for.

Jyoti: I don't think I was wrong (she said giving a look towards us, making a gesture with her hands). Love is referred to as love only when your mental status is totally uncrowned by any other thing, but if it's been under some disorder like being drunk, then the activities you do are referred to as inhuman and totally illegal. So let's get back to the normal life and discuss love being appreciated by people surrounding us, as I don't want someone to beat you over your definition of love.

Mayank interrupted.

Mayank: Beat?

Jyoti: Yeah beat! If you'd tell someone that an alcoholic is experiencing the highest form of love, then they would certainly beat you. Anyway, how would you define love? (She asked Mayank rocking her chin upward towards him.)

Mayank was caught unawares as we all turned towards him.

Mayank: But how would I know?

Jyoti: Don't you have a girlfriend?

Mayank: Yeah, I have.

I: For the last five years!

Jyoti: Five years! Really? Then you must have experienced real feelings of being in love. Please share your experiences so we can get to know some more intense feelings for the biggest illusion.

Mayank: I…

The streetlight suddenly went off and getting scared I held Mayank's hand as there was not even a single thing I could see in the darkness. Instantly, Mayank switched on the light of his phone.

Jyoti: Wait a minute, I'll bring a candle.

She went down the steps towards the river.

I: What time is it?

Baba: It's two.

Mayank too replied the same.

I: How come you know the time without looking at the clock?

I got scared as he was correct.

Baba: Every night there is a power cut at two.

I was relieved. Jyoti returned with a candle in her hand.

She kept the candle on the window of the shop, in front of which we were sitting.

Jyoti: So, Mayank you were trying to say something. Carry on.

Mayank: Yeah, but I don't know how and where to start.

Jyoti: Okay, let's do something for you. You close your eyes and just start saying whatever you feel. We'll stay quiet. Pretend like no one's around you.

Mayank closed his eyes.

Mayank: I don't know what it feels, but the biggest change love has caused is that it has ended the feeling of selfishness. Whenever we are together, I don't have any other wish. I feel complete. I just don't want a single extra thing in this world than finding her beside me. And I hate the moment she leaves me; it seems like I'm left alone. But when she smiles looking back at me, I get out of the sadness and it makes me wait eagerly for the next time we'll meet. As she holds my hand, the feeling is inexpressible, because at that moment I can't feel anything beyond the magical touch of her fingers. My eyes close when she kisses me. When I hug her, I feel I'm in possession of the whole world, as I consider her my world. I become restless and uncomfortable every second if something is wrong with her. I can't see anyone beyond her. Wherever I am, she's always on my mind.

Every time she smiles, I consider a million dollars earned, and also there are times when I feel like giving a million dollars just to see her smiling. And it seems like someone has taken the life out of me when she's struggling with the smallest bit of sadness.

Mayank deepened his breath and held it long, rocking his body with the most sincere smile on his face. I looked at Jyoti, rather all three of us looked at each other without saying anything. He continued.

Mayank: This is what happens to me when I see her: an unexpected smile reflects on my face without my consent. My eyes close, heart gets numb and I am not able to move any part of my body for a while. The feeling of being with her gives me a disorder, maybe because god wants me to know that this is your limit and your destiny, so never try to change it else you'd not be able to move any part of your body. I hope everybody realizes their destinies as well.

Mayank opened his eyes smiling and blushing at the same moment. Jyoti clapped her hands silently. Baba was also smiling, nodding his head in approval, though I don't know what he was approving. I, for that matter, had never seen this side of him – Baba Mayank.

Jyoti: Don't just smile, Narendra; we expect a clarification of love from you. Though they were brought to me, you must be having your own thoughts on the matter.

Baba hesitated but began slowly.

Baba: Love is such a vast feeling that it can never be defined, but if you insist, I'll try to embrace it in words. Let's talk about love between a man and a woman. I do not consider it a relation of just merely involving two bodies, but a relation of the mind and the heart. As to be in love, both need to understand one another's needs and sentiments. Expectations should be high, but the other person should know each and every bit of what you expect, so he/she can try to always keep your never-ending confidence and love alive. And yes, making love is one major factor here that enhances the feeling of being together; it gives you the closest moments to embrace the beauty of your love. Making love is one of the moments when everything seems dull, apart from the beauty of your partner. Besides, these feelings cannot be expressed in words…

Baba: Now, we should talk about the love for one's parents. It's something we can't repay, but through good deeds and showing the same love and affection towards them is the way we can at least be in the queue of ending our lives without regret. The feeling that you give to your parents just by listening to their query is the biggest achievement for them. They don't want much, but just to treat their children exactly the same way they used to do in their childhood. Everyone here knows how parents are treated as a child gets older; I just don't understand why a person can't treat their parents the same way through this short lifespan. I mean, you used to nod in approval about everything you were asked to do while you were a kid, then why can't you obey the simple rule through life just to keep your creators happy! Does common sense decline with age? We all know our childhood was amazing and in that beautiful phase we used to say yes to everything our parents asked us to do, then I question, why, I mean why a person can't obey those simple rules during the rest of one's life. It won't cost us much, but just a feeling of seeing our parents happy. Can't we do even this much for them?

Baba was almost in tears. Jyoti patted his back asking me with an indication to come and do the same as I and Mayank got speechless over the beautiful words he had just spoken. I went closer to Baba and did the same by patting his back. Baba regained his composure and asked me to sit down. He wasn't done yet.

Baba: I am not asking for much, but just a small request to keep your parents happy. No one has to do anything much but just keep their minds open for everything that a parent is asking them to do. If one can't obey them, then at least try to make the reason clear to them. It certainly will contribute to peace and will also make the world a better place to live in. Upbringing would become easier as the respectful rituals of every family would become the same. And, most importantly, people would be able to define love in a much easier way. Apart from everything, love is something that you make your parents feel, or the feeling they get when you show your respect and obedience.

Pin drop silence. Each one of us was busy in refining his or her thoughts. He gave a totally different note that is to be added to the column of love. I was happy to learn this new perspective and the way to achieve it.

I: I'll certainly follow the same, and will tell people the awesomeness of being the follower of this known yet undiscovered fact.

I said this out of the excitement of being enlightened.

Jyoti: I wish you could do what you want to. I want to spread this truth all over the world. Everyone wants to go to heaven, but nobody knows how they can. Count me in if you ever have an idea how to spread it…I would love to come along the path of trying to enlighten people.

Baba: I am really sorry for taking the conversation to a totally different direction.

Jyoti: Narendra, this is the most important direction, and I wonder why we didn't take it earlier to make these beautiful souls understand the real truth of being alive.

I was nodding in approval by rocking my head very fast, and was noticed by Jyoti.

Jyoti: Seems like you've got things right and are trying to feed them in your mind. So why don't you give us the privilege to trace your words? We'd love to get it through your way.

Mayank: Come on man, you can do it. If I can, then why can't you?

I: Did I say that am not willing to?

After closing my eyes and deepening my breath, I started speaking without giving it a second thought.

I: It's nothing complicated, but simple and straight. According to me, 'love is the way you are'. It's your way of doing things. If you can look at everything lovingly, then the whole world becomes beautiful for you. Love is to create an aura of happiness around you, all the time. Love is when you have a loving family; a brother who cares, a sister who you can count on no matter what the situation is, and also to share secrets with, a mother who'd do anything to keep the children happy and together, and most importantly, a father you barely see because he's just unimaginably busy working to keep his family together.

Love is a feeling that occurs when you think nothing more can be done or you've lost all your hope and suddenly the person beside you says 'Am I not there with you?' And understands the right way, making things better for you, keeping his own desires and needs aside, just to see you happy. To love someone isn't that easy, but it means to be willing to risk your life for that person, to be with them in good and bad times, and to always put their needs above yours. Love is humble and caring, giving and sharing, patient and tender, pure and full, selfless and thoughtful, soft and tough, and incredible and beyond imagination. I tried, but defining it only in some words is not fair as every word in the dictionary defines it in some or the other way and every move of a Homo sapien is linked with a feeling of love in different ways. I think I can't summarize it in a better way.

Jyoti: I think everyone here is a master of beautiful thoughts. I mean everyone is embracing it so beautifully like they've been teaching it in different sections. I am glad that the three of us tried to embrace love and all of us took it in totally different directions, making it more interesting. And were you really asking me what love is? (She looked at me) You know it better than I could have ever put. You say 'love is the way you are'; I mean, what could be a more simplified way to simplify love. I'd say you know it better than me, and now I'd love to take a class to simplify life from all three of you.

All of us laughed.

There was silence, but this time, I was relaxed as I could see Jyoti and Baba pondering over my words. Mayank was looking towards the sky; don't know what he was trying to do. I decided to break the silence.

I: You insisted all of us to describe what love is in our words, now can we get yours?

Baba and Mayank nodded at her.

Jyoti: I'd certainly do it for you, but I am confused about where I should start. I mean, you guys haven't left much for me to say. I can only sum up the situations where you find it in extreme emotions, which can make you feel the essence of love. Let me simplify it with a situation. It is at the moment you make love to your partner. It isn't like making love with anyone, but just with someone specific that you adore from the deepest sensations of your heart. I am adding the word specific because he/she would be the only one you can feel to the fullest. You also expect the same in return. These moments are the one when your feelings are at the optimum level. In these moments, you don't think much, but just close your eyes feeling the essence of the closeness of your better half and let it flow. People complicate it by saying that the word is small but it's difficult to understand. I mean, you've to give your best in everything you do, and then I don't know how it can be difficult?

And sometimes you also have to break away from things, just to see what happens. I would recommend you to have a very few people in your life as your lifelines. Everyone should have them, and if you don't, then you should make a few; choose them wisely. Go for those who make you laugh and laugh for you, who make you cry and cry for you. Go for the one who stands by you, whatever may be the situation or reason. And, you certainly can find them in the crowd. Love isn't just giving, but also receiving, though it should not be a compulsion on the part of the other. It isn't a mediocrity, but eternity.

People in a relationship say 'love hurts'. But according to me, it never does; rather it's the expectation that hurts, and it certainly happens with a person who's expecting a lot without even letting the other one know about what he feels.

Okay, let me try to elaborate it with a different perspective. Let me give you the words that for the first time made me realize its depth. It was not from someone I didn't know, but my own grandfather. It was the time when I had just entered my teenage years. We used to go for a walk every day after dinner. On one such walk, I asked him what love was? He gave me a shock by saying 'your grandmother'. It made me curious. And this is what he said. It's nothing, but a woman who surrounds your world. The one who's there in everything you do. She's someone who understands you and trusts you being her caretaker, and also rejoices sacrificing anything for you. She understands your mood almost all the time and changes hers accordingly. A woman taking care of your life is an impression of how you are going to deal with it. In spite of every soul you encounter, she's the only one who will define your every day.

So this is how he defined it. Everyone has different perceptions according to their interests. Some say their better half is love, like my grandfather. Some people are just the opposite; they love themselves more than anything. Some people love their work and they don't want anything to distract them, like one playing football, or the one who sings, or the one who thinks he's born to travel around the world. Different people, different interests, different explanations and different beliefs, and accordingly different amendments in their different truths, but, above all, love remains the same.

Loving something or someone is accepting the way they are and appreciating their flaws. *Being loved* is being in the center of unimaginable affection that gets you away from the mediocrity of the normal world. *Being in love* is a feeling you cannot experience alone, but is to be felt together. And, being in love is the biggest gift that god presents one with. Now don't indulge in its search; it itself will reach you. Just be patient, rather wait and watch.

Jyoti finished her speech and there was pin drop silence. Mayank and I looked at each other. But Baba looked down, his eyes closed and murmuring.

Long pause. No one tried to say anything, but Jyoti was smiling at me.

"Do you know what exactly wisdom is?"

I just happened to blurt out these words and Baba seemed to look at me in disbelief. I looked back at him wondering what he was trying to suggest.

"You're ruining my night," he finally said.

Mayank and Jyoti laughed.

"Narendra, you can go and sleep…now I am comfortable with these pupils."

Without giving it another thought, Baba stood up like a rocket and bent over me to say goodbye with a hug and did the same to Mayank. He smiled at Jyoti.

"I knew you were waiting for me to give you this assurance. I hope you'll thank me for letting you sleep. Making him understand what wisdom is will continue up to daybreak for sure."

"You guys will do something really unexpectedly well," saying this, he smiled and began walking down the street.

"What's the time?" Jyoti asked.

"Ten past three," Mayank said almost in shock.

Ignoring Mayank, Jyoti said, "We can go to Baba Aliyanka."

Interrupting her, I said, "Aliyanka, what kind of a name is this?"

"Yeah, he isn't Indian, but he lives in a cottage beside the river on a big rock and wakes up at three. We can't find anyone more knowledgeable than him in the surroundings. And, we can only find him till four, after which he leaves his cottage and goes up into the mountains to meditate."

"So we still have half an hour," I interrupted.

"Yeah, it's the best time to meet him."

"Should we leave for his cottage?" Jyoti queried.

"I can't make it," Mayank said firmly.

"You can leave for the hotel and rest, he'll be back in two hours," Jyoti said without my consent. I nodded, a little hesitant.

Things were going too fast and I was not able to think. As Jyoti stood, she blew her candle off and asked me to walk behind her. I didn't have any choice but to follow her. Mayank realized what was going on and he called me back. I went up to him and he said,

"Share your location on WhatsApp when you reach there, and also give me a call if you have any issues. You turn around; I'll see you from here till you disappear. Meet you at the hotel," Mayank said this a little louder. Perhaps he wanted Jyoti to hear him. Jyoti started walking towards the river, and I followed her without any hesitation. This time, we were in total darkness. A cold shiver went through my body, making me still, freezing my feet on the ground as I heard the roar of the Ganges. A different feeling came over me as I had never been close to a vast water body at such a time. And, my weakness, the phobia of water came over me. I wondered what would happen if I slipped and fell.

The flight of steps ended and we reached the riverside.

"It's a full moon night, so don't get worried, we'll find our way," she said interrupting my thoughts. And yes, River Ganges was looking beautiful. Its surface was shining like silver and the flowing waves made it seem like radium. I stopped for a moment to see the spectacular sight. We started walking towards the left on the banks full of sand. I realized we were really close to the river and were going to cross a narrow path between a huge rock and the Ganges.

Jyoti crossed it by putting one step first, then the other.

"Put your step exactly in the middle and I'll catch you when you jump."

Gathering all my courage, I did as I was told. I tried looking for something to hold on to, but found nothing. I shouted for help as Jyoti grasped my shoulder. I landed shivering. Standing there and looking at the Ganges, I realized how close to the end I was. Jyoti patted my back. I saw a phone's light dancing on the Lakshman Jhula. And my phone buzzed. Oh, damn it, my phone.

Mayank was calling me.

"Are you fine?" These were his first words in a fearful voice.

"Yeah I am," I replied calmly, as I didn't want to go back.

"Then why did you shout?" he queried.

"Just to make you aware that I am alive," I laughed to assure him of my wellbeing. He hung up and I started following Jyoti.

"We've to go there," she said pointing to a dim light around a couple of hundred steps to our right.

"Don't speak much in front of him, but just listen to his words. Maybe you won't understand them right away, but trust me, when you'll recall them, you'll get to know what exactly they mean. He's a very sensitive human who changes your words which are wrong according to you and manipulates them accordingly, in a way that would seem totally different. Almost everyone around this place knows him and respects him. He won't ask you anything, but will just explain things, so keep your ears open. Now you need to help me in climbing up this short-cut.

She climbed halfway and needed my support, so I heaved her upwards over the rock. I did the same and yes, she helped me by pulling me with all the energy she had. I almost laughed having the glimpse of her face with her closed eyes and stretched lips. She looked like an angry monkey, but with closed eyes.

"At last we've reached," she said in a satisfied tone.

I looked up panting. There was nobody near the cottage, but a small bulb was hanging over the door. Jyoti asked me what time it was.

"It's 3:23!" I exclaimed, "This was a night trek," I said pointing to the riverside.

"I've done it a lot of times and sometimes fifty times more than this," Jyoti said rocking her head for teasing me.

"Fifty times!" I exclaimed with wide eyes. "But where did you go?"

"I, along with three more people, had trekked to Neelkanth Temple. We started around half past two in the morning and reached there at seven. Isn't that cool?" she laughed.

"No, not at all. It sounds horrifying," I said very sincerely.

Suddenly she pointed towards an old man coming up a few steps.

"That's Baba Aliyanka's presence. He must have gone for a bath."

"Why did we come trekking if there are steps to get here?" I said a bit annoyed.

"It would have taken us longer and we would have missed him."

As Baba came closer, Jyoti bent with her hands joined to wish him the beautiful essence of morning and I too went to touch his feet for which in return he said, "You will glow."

I keenly watched him as he placed his towel on the rope. He was stiff and looked around seventy, judging by the colour of his hair. But what was extremely surprising was the glow of his face. Without his hair he wouldn't seem a day older than forty. I was very confused about his age.

Baba Aliyanka: Sit! (He said pointing towards a rock which maybe he or someone else has crafted like a chair.) What would you like to have, water or fruits?

Jyoti asked for water and I refused both.

Jyoti: We just want a little time of yours as he is a boy from Delhi who came to me with Narendra for clarifying his doubts about life and love. He's really very intense and understands them in an amazing manner.

Baba Aliyanka interrupted.

Baba Aliyanka: Were his words heavy for your knowledge?

Jyoti: I tried my best, but as he asked about wisdom, I didn't give it a second thought and brought him to you.

Baba Aliyanka: So my friend, I won't waste time by asking you what wisdom is, but would just tell you that it is there in your every move. Yes, every move.

I got confused, I don't know whether by his knowledge or his agility. As I asked him the question, he did three things very swiftly: he gave a glass of water to Jyoti, brought a chair for himself, and kept a fruit basket in front of us.

I: Every move?

I exclaimed with a raised eyebrow.

Baba Aliyanka: Yes, my friend, 'everything' I mentioned. The way you cried for help when you slipped into the river a few minutes back shows your wisdom. Okay, tell me why did you shout?

I: I shouted for help as it is human nature to shout and let people know if they are going through some pain.

Baba Aliyanka: You are right. But you didn't notice that this is your wisdom. Wisdom to know that if you are in danger and you shout, you can get out of that danger. Wisdom to know how you can save yourself by involving others.

I was stunned with the amazing example he had crafted to make me realize the wisdom I apply in my day to day life to save myself from different threats. I felt very calm and astonished at the same time.

Baba Aliyanka: Okay tell me, what do you think I did when I heard you shouting?

I: Well, you must have first tried to find out what the matter was.

Baba Aliyanka: Okay, let me tell you. I was standing with half of my body in water when I heard you shout. Instead of panicking, I stood still and tried to ignore any other sound but the sound of a human or a body flowing or trying to swim in water, because according to my wisdom, if a person shouts for help at this hour of night, there is a chance he is drowning. I didn't hear any splashing in the water, so I knew you were safe. This, according to me, is wisdom; knowing what to do at a specific time and when it is needed most.

Baba rendered me speechless by his simple everyday examples. Was Baba a different person or is wisdom really so common to us that we take it for granted?

Interrupting my thoughts, Baba continued: You lack wisdom. How? I should tell you. You came here as my student, and when I asked you to choose between water or fruits, you chose neither. And, to my best knowledge, if you've been offered something from an elder, specifically a teacher, then refusing is lack of wisdom. You are simply demeaning him. Though I can understand your thought process, but still, these are the basic things a person so gentlemanly like you should know.

Was he right? I thought as I recalled similar words from my professor Mr. K. K. Gupta. The Professor and Baba Aliyanka must be of the same age with the same knowledge.

Baba Aliyanka: Whatever you are thinking at this moment is absolutely right. Okay, let me tell you, though I can't be hundred percent correct, but I can say that you are thinking of some old man whose words were similar to mine. Am I correct?

I: Absolutely! But how did you know?

Baba Aliyanka: Though this was not wisdom, instances like these come from experiences.

I: But how did you know that I was thinking about an old man's words?

Baba Aliyanka: Because words bearing such a sound knowledge can't be said by a budding star like you.

I: Okay, but apart from this example, what do you call wisdom?

Baba Aliyanka: Wisdom is to live till you die.

Interrupting him, I said: Sorry to interrupt you, but everyone is running after money, as everyone wants to become rich.

Without letting me complete my question, he interrupted me with a request to share a knowledgeable thought.

Baba Aliyanka: Today I am sharing with you the greatest words of a great soul:

You can never get rich without spending something; but if you really want to get rich, then spend on travelling.

So according to this beautiful soul, becoming rich is the easiest thing. Believe me, when you'll start spending your money on travelling, then you shall get richer in experiences. And, the biggest wisdom is the curiosity of knowing something followed by the action for achieving it. Trust the Almighty for giving it all for free, just by being a traveller. I don't think there can be a simpler way than to just pack your bags and get started for *anywhere*.

I said 'wisdom is to live till you die', so here, living is being referred to as travelling.

Let me make it simpler for you. You are here because you were travelling, and you are gaining knowledge, again because you are travelling. Here you are gaining experiences for life. This wouldn't have happened if you had been at home. I am not saying I know more than you, but of course, experience counts as I must have definitely travelled more than you.

All three of us giggled as Baba Aliyanka said this with a smile.

I tried to say something as I lifted my hand a little and was just opening my lips, but was stopped by Baba.

Baba Aliyanka: I am running out of time, so I request you to only listen and keep your doubts alive till we meet again. I mean if we ever meet again.

I was bewildered by his words. I mean, was he trying to stop me from asking the difficult questions I had, or did he really want to impart the amazing sense of knowledge and experience he had in the short span of time we were together. I decided to quietly listen and concentrate.

Baba Aliyanka: Knowledge, something we all are aware of. From where does it start? Knowledge begins with the fear of god taught by our parents. And, as we talk about wisdom, I should say it starts with honesty about everything around you, and most importantly, to oneself. Honesty isn't something to be described, but an activity that a mind can perform by itself, without being guided by any external factors.

…And, knowledge is the reality to know that you eventually will die.

…Wisdom allows you to look beyond your selfishness, so it eventually becomes service before self. Giving away is not the thing, but giving for betterment of others is. Giving can be classified in different types: it may be giving away some of the best knowledge you have or any materialistic thing that you believe will help the other person. But what I believe in the most and above amongst anything else…is teaching. Give him something materialistic and he'll thank you for the time being; but teach him to become the messenger of god, for helping him deal with a specific thing for his whole life.

I gave a puzzled look. Aliyanka cleared his throat, rocking his head from left to right, and then a little upwards stretching it.

Baba Aliyanka: To make my last words clear, I use a very common saying: 'Give a man a fish and you feed him for a day; teach a man to fish and you feed him for life.'

According to a priest like me, who doesn't want to indulge with the goings on of the world, wisdom is peace. Do not mistake peace with the calmness of your surroundings. What it actually means is the calmness of your emotions, and most importantly, the ending of your needs resulting in the calmness of your mind. I said ending your needs, mind it. If you are not bothered about a single thing, human being or activity in the world, then I'll call it peace; but it doesn't mean that every time, you have to be neutral. If you see someone sad, you should empathise, making him feel the best you can; and if you find someone happy, then again, you should feel his joy and add to it. This doesn't mean that you have to be in the same emotion for a long time, but as soon as you leave the person, you also have to leave the emotion behind. It's one of the toughest things to be practiced by any human living a normal life, but if he achieves it, then he certainly can be assumed to be on the path of enlightenment. Enlightenment of getting closer to God and knowing oneself.

…Wisdom is to walk forward, whatever may come. Even if a person is crawling, he is technically moving forward. So to keep oneself in touch with wisdom, he should keep doing something or the other that makes today better than yesterday.

Now at this moment, I can assure that you are practicing wisdom. How, you'd ask? Just by simply listening to me. Listening to others is a form of wisdom that anyone in the world can perform with perfection.

People say, being satisfied with what you have is wisdom. But no, wisdom is to live happily with what you have and strive for the next level without getting hurt with setbacks or failures which may come along the way. Dreaming for the best is the asset of your wisdom.

He was interrupted by the morning's very first chirruping of birds. Aliyanka became alert with the sound and looked at his right towards the peak of a mountain far away from us. I realized that he certainly was looking at the dimmest ray of sunlight which can only be seen if one observes it keenly.

Looking at me like an observer, Aliyanka said: Okay, I tried to make my best effort, so are you ready to pay me for the same?

I was shocked as I did not have my wallet with me. Then I instantly realized that he wouldn't ask for money, but would ask me something from what he had taught me.

I: Okay.

I was a little hesitant though.

Aliyanka: You noticed I stopped in between. So can you tell me why I did that?

Without hesitation I said: Yes, as according to me, the sound of the birds is an alarm for you and to confirm their perfect timing, you looked for the sun's rays.

Aliyanka: I won't coat the appreciation for you in words. But I appreciate that you listened to every word. I can assume that you'd have understood everything I tried to teach you.

He stood up and went into his cottage. Instantly he came back with his brass thurible.

Aliyanka: I appreciate your efforts to come and meet me. I hope I ended giving you something appreciable. Also remember, appreciating others and oneself is also wisdom. Wisdom is hidden in every move. So don't get worried and yes, think about things deeply. It was nice meeting you, and Jyoti I am sorry that you couldn't sleep tonight. Thank her for her efforts. Let's see if we can meet again.

He said this to me with the brightest smile, before he turned around and went down the steps.

Nothing changed, and I kept sitting without saying anything, staring at Aliyanka's empty chair. I realized that I was almost numb.

And, sorry I was wrong, as everything changed. Yes, everything. I tried to lift my hand, but I wasn't able to, so I left it the way it was and gave my body time. I closed my eyes and rocked my head upwards, deepening the amazing sound of the flowing river. I was not even bothered about Jyoti and she remained silent as well.

"Bam Bam Bhole."

These were the words which interrupted my silence. I opened my eyes and found Aliyanka chanting, moving his hands up and down.

"What is this, it's morning!" I exclaimed shocked.

"Yes it is. So should we leave?" Jyoti asked as she got up.

"Yeah, but where would you go, as you can't even sleep now?" I showed my genuine concern as I was worried about her.

"You don't get worried, I'll go to a friend's cottage up there for a nap," she said pointing towards the high peak in front of us.

I thought of asking about the friend, but kept quiet. She started walking down the steps and I followed her without any questions, as my body seemed to have returned to normalcy from the state of being numb.

"These steps seem unending," I said exhausted.

"See, didn't I tell you about them? They are tiring because they're zig zag. That allows a person to tone their calf muscles. And also, they are a deterrent and keep Baba and his cottage secluded. People hardly come up these steep steps."

At last we reached the riverside. I turned around and tried to look at the cottage where I had gained profound truths of life.

"You should leave now," Jyoti said and sounded rather emotional.

"Yes, it's high time. I don't know how to thank you and make you believe that you became the person who imparted the most important truths on how to live and enjoy this beautiful life."

I touched her feet, being thankful. She caressed my head and cupping my face said, "You are one of the amazing souls I have met. You have the power to change the world because you have patience and zest and the power to listen to the world. As Aliyanka had said, 'If you have the power to listen, then you'll certainly get the power to change'. Good luck, my son. May god shower his best on you."

Her words were so touching that I almost had tears in my eyes. She wiped my eyes, asking me to leave. I started walking without looking back. The mixed feelings were making my sadness more intense, asking me to stop and look back, but wisdom asked me to move forward. I climbed the stairs and started walking towards my left to cross the river. I felt sad, but on the other hand, I felt strong and tough. Reaching the Lakshman Jhula, I stopped in the middle as I found Jyoti sitting on the riverside with her half bent legs hugged by her hands over which she rested her chin. She looked at me waving her hand. I started for the hotel. I was continuously thinking about the deeply profound words of Baba Aliyanka. They had gone down my heart and left their mark. I mean, they made me feel positive and I felt I could face anything at that moment. As I reached the hotel, the sun rays illuminated the huge mountains. I gaped at the magnificent sight from my balcony and knocked on the door. Mayank opened the door instantly.

"How did you hear me knocking? You are usually as good as dead when you sleep!"

"I was extremely worried about you. I tried to sleep, but could not."

He asked me about what had happened, but I was too tired to give any heed to his words. Taking off my shoes, I threw myself on the bed and closed my eyes. I was asleep within seconds.

"Who's calling me at this hour," I muttered as my phone was continuously ringing for the past five minutes. I looked for the phone with my hand, my eyes still closed. I finally found it and saw that it was Tushinder calling me. But why was he calling me this early? I looked at the clock and saw that it was 9.23 a.m.

He had called to remind me that I was to go for a ride with him after two days. I assured him I'd be there and hung up. I wanted to go back to sleep desperately. As I drifted off to sleep, I suddenly felt someone pulling at my pants.

"It's noon, will you please wake up so we can go somewhere for breakfast?" screamed Mayank.

In spite of getting angry, I didn't react. Mayank left for the German Bakery in a huff. As he banged the door, I looked at the time again. It was 9:37.

This time, I gave up trying to get some sleep and went to the bathroom. I picked up my pen and diary. I realized that my inner self had made me pick up the diary. I remembered Aliyanka's face and smiled at the thought of my wisdom. Looking down at the diary, it seemed to be the oldest friend I had.

I left the keys at the counter and headed to the German café myself. When I reached, I realized that I had left my phone in the room.

I couldn't find Mayank anywhere in the café, so I decided to go to a less crowded place. Crossing the Lakshman Jhula, I turned to the direction where I had spent my whole night. I found a beautifully decorated café's entrance. The board read 'Buddha Café' and one had to go up a narrow flight of stairs. It was on the second floor. The café was less crowded and it gave me the feeling of the existence of purity. A white man smiled at me while his wife waved. A person was sitting in the corner with his Mac. Maybe he was concentrating on the beauty of his words. I went out into the balcony, putting my diary on the table.

Resting my hands on the railing of the balcony, I took long deep breaths, letting the oxygen reach my lungs and give a spark to my brain, which would activate the hidden voice entrapped in my fingers.

Sitting down, I raised my hand to call the waiter. Ordering a ginger lemon tea and a Nutella pancake, I opened a fresh page in my diary. The waiter brought the tea instantly and I took advantage of the early drink.

Stirring the spoon reflected my whirring mind and tapping it made me realize that yes, it would work. After a sip, I took the pen and without saying anything, looking at the peak in front of me, I penned the words coming from my mind.

Sitting beside the Ganges is an opportunity,
That everyone gets, but not the witty,

Here in Buddha Café I realized,
As to why a person gets hypnotized,

Places like this are still there in the world,
Where a person comes and his life gets curled,

With a palatable ginger lemon tea on my table,
The purpose of life seems perceptible,

So what exactly I've decided,
Is something that would make it seem bighted,

But this is what a very few know,
As you get what you want only after playing the bow,
As you get what you want only after playing the bow...

I looked up to find the pancake waiting for me which I proceeded to devour with great pleasure. Paying the bill, I walked back to find Mayank sitting in the balcony, looking angry.

"Hey brother, how have you been? It's one p.m. Do you realize how long I've been waiting for you?

"It's fine, you woke me up at twelve and I am here at one." I laughed loudly and he joined me sheepishly. We packed our bags as Mayank had already gotten the tickets for a bus to Delhi that was going to leave at 2:30.

Picking up his bag, Mayank asked me to come downstairs to the reception where he'd be waiting for me. Taking my bag, I followed him just after he passed the lobby and found Manaka running towards her room's door. Was she running to see me? This thought made me numb for a moment and as she was standing behind the netted door, I asked about her roommate. She had gone out for lunch, Manaka said in the most innocent manner. She unbolted the door, but didn't push it open. Baba Aliyanka, Narendra and Jyoti flashed in front of my eyes, but I continued to open the door by pulling it. I grabbed her waist with my left hand. She closed her eyes and started breathing heavily. This time, Baba Aliyanka flashed through my mind, to which I loosened the grip over her waist. She opened her eyes.

"Fuck the wisdom," I said loudly and tightened the grip of my palm over her waist pulling her closer and started kissing her instantly. This time I wasn't shocked, but yes, her fingers were in my hair. I dropped the bag and held her more tightly with both my hands.

It is said that when you are way happier than what you should be in a situation, god brings you back. My phone rang. The screen flashed 'Mayank'. This was the moment my phone was snatched by none other than Manaka. Instead of keeping it with her, she threw it on my bag. I was offended and pushed her away. I grabbed the phone and the bag.

"I've to leave now," I said without showing any anger and turned my back towards her.

"Fuck off, you can never be a man with a heart," were the words I heard. She was saying something more, but it was time to leave. Wisdom was to leave the place right at that moment, I said to myself and shouted to Mayank to come out to the entrance of the hotel. Hiring an auto, we reached the bus stand. After a quick lunch, we boarded the bus. I narrated the events of the night leisurely to Mayank as we made our way home.

Reaching home, I touched my mother's feet. She hugged me as though I was back from some war. There was a sense of fear in the calmness of having me in her arms. I didn't eat anything, but went to sleep with the hope of starting a new life.

With this, I hoped that I'd live *'the life of my dreams'*.

I went through the things left in my internship.

I thought things would be easier and life would smoothen itself. But things went for a toss.

Every night it became tough for me to sleep, thoughts proceeded to ruin my nights. But these went in for the making of a new me.

I spoke with Mayank to know if he was also going through anything like this. No, he was as normal as he used to be, a person who wanted to see people dancing on Saturdays.

I took it differently, thinking if it was the impact of Aliyanka's words, and maybe I was searching for wisdom. Wisdom for my life, what I had to do, things for which I have to excel in my life.

I started asking my friends and people who knew me well about what I was good at. Before asking them, I was confused, but now I was furious about asking them at all.

After a few days, I was sitting at a café waiting for a friend. Thoughts wandered, and a scene from the past hour ran through my mind.

It pinched me hard, though it was a part of the normal life we lead.

It was a beggar whom I saw while driving through Nehru Place. He was sitting on the road's divider crossing his legs with a car's wheel cover kept in his front. I had seen him many times, wandering around the same place, sleeping by the roadside almost every morning. But that was the only day that I realized that I saw him almost every day with an unconscious mind.

But why did he come to my mind was a question backed by why did he keep that car's wheel cover in front of him. Was he selling it, or did he steal it from somewhere and wanted to make some money out of it?

I immediately called Ankit to tell him not to bring his car tomorrow and that I will pick him up for college the next day.

I was all set to answer Ankit's questions for the same, and was preparing my mind to make myself sit with a person on the roadside till he answered me.

Handing over the car to Deovrat and settling myself on the back seat, I made them understand my urge, but their only concern were the traffic policemen. I didn't pay heed to their queries and rather was more worried about meeting the person.

Reaching there, we found him sleeping on the footpath on the other end, sitting only fifty steps away from the police interceptor. I jumped out of the car as we were at a red light.

When I saw him, the first reaction was surprise. He was filthy, exactly like he looked from a distance. I saw Deovrat parking the car besides the interceptor and in some conversation with the policeman. I ignored him and moved on.

It was difficult for me to get the courage to speak to him; besides, it seemed he was fast asleep.

"Bhaiya," I gathered some courage and spoke up.

He turned, and to my shock, almost jumped and sat up as soon as he realized I was speaking to him.

Before I could have said anything else, he started searching for something in his blanket that he had put under his head to make it his pillow.

What was he searching for, I wondered. I also moved a step back, to ensure that he didn't even think of harming me in any way. Meanwhile, my eye caught a glimpse of the car's wheel cover that he might not have sold yesterday.

The sound of a fizz suddenly pierced my thoughts; he was spraying a perfume that he had pulled out from his blanket.

I smiled, and being carried away with his innocence, asked his name.

"Beggar," he replied with ease, giving me a shock.

"What?! What kind of a name is that?" I asked, a little sad.

This is what people have called me ever since I remember.

I was very stunned with his answer. There was no denying the fact that he was very clear about his thoughts and words.

"You want to buy this?" he asked pointing to the wheel cover.

"Yes, but how did you know?" I said, just to extend the conversation.

"But I will not charge you less than 150 rupees." He made it clear with one statement.

"I will give you 200 rupees for this, but before that, you have to answer a few questions," I said, trying to strike a sort of a deal.

"Give me a cigarette, and I'll answer everything," pat came his reply.

"I don't smoke," I stated looking at Ankit, just in case he was not going to answer me without his needs.

"Ok, then give me one when you cross this place the next time. I know you cross by frequently. I saw you looking at the wheel cover yesterday while snailing through the traffic," he said.

"Why did you steal it?" I said as he looked at the wheel cover. "Do you have any need of doing it?"

"This is the only thing I can do to make people talk to me. Nobody talks to me if I don't have anything. I only keep this (he said pointing towards the perfume bottle he had) so I won't smell bad to the ones who talk to me. I love it, and that's why I do it. I don't get tired searching for things that eventually make me happy."

The most common words, I thought to myself. I gave him three hundred rupees, leaving him with the wheel cover.

"When will you come back?" he shouted.

"Very soon," I said with a smile.

☀

"I don't get tired searching for things that eventually make me smile," were the words that echoed in my mind again and again. These words were like caffeine to my sleep. They were pinching me, letting me use my mind to think hard about what was missing from my life that would give me ample happiness that I needed.

Then I recalled my words in Manaka's voice, "Our fingers have the power to think like our mind."

Is it writing? I thought to myself. I gave it a thought and realized that when I had tried to write a novel, for which I was chasing experiences, I was never tired. Though it was something else that both the times I did not find the story appropriate and quit it midway.

Should I give it another try? It was a moment that almost shook me, but I was moved by the thought.

I started writing the very same day, but soon the interest in its regularity began to fade again.

There came the dreadful night when I left every other thing to make time for my writing.

And here today, I complete it for you, and ask you to ask yourself: What is that one thing and take time for the same to become what you ever wished for.

Believe me, if it happened for me, it certainly will happen for **YOU**.

Recommended Reading

Her Last Wish
Ajay K Pandey

His father's over expectations only ruined his self-confidence further with each failure. A ray of hope walked into his life as his wife. Everything is going per plan, when he finds out that she does not have much time to live and takes it upon himself to fight all odds – even his family, if need be – to help her fight her medical condition.

Her Last Wish is an inspiring story of love, relationships and sacrifice.

Ajay is the bestselling author of *You are the Best Wife* and has won many hearts with his writing. He is also actively involved in working for social causes.

ISBN: 978-9382665878; Price: 175/-; Pages: 208; Binding: Paperback.

You are my Reason to Smile
Arpit Vageria

Ranbir is a dreamer. He has a well-paying job, is a good lover, an ideal son, but he is not happy. Because his true calling is not in the corporate; it's in writing. Amidst all this confusion, Pihu Sharma enters his life – his first ever fan, who seems to be head over heels in love with him. Join Ranbir as he makes his way through a world that kills for money and dies for love.

Arpit Vageria is a bestselling author of *I Still Think About You*. He also writes for the Indian television industry, and enjoys road trips, singing, playing pranks and adventurous sports.

ISBN: 978-9382665885; Price: 175/-; Pages: 184; Binding: Paperback.

Finding Juliet
Toffee

Arjun is an incredibly nice guy who believes in true love and is waiting for it with open arms. He falls in love, not once or twice, but thrice. And every single time, is left heartbroken. His only pillar of strength through this is his childhood friend Anjali.

Then he meets Krish, who enlightens him about women and changes his life forever. Join Arjun as he tries to figure out women and discovers the meaning of love, lust and life.

Toffee is a simple guy who loves the complications of life. Through books, he wants to share beautiful stories, reach out to people and touch their hearts.

ISBN: 978-9382665854; Price: 195/-; Pages: 224; Binding: Paperback.

Colorful Notions
Mohit Goyal

Would you give up your high-paying job and comfortable personal life to drive ten thousand kilometers across India? Just for fun!

Three twenty-somethings dare to do just that! While the two boys take turns to drive, the girl gives voice-over as they record their entire journey on a handy cam. Join a journey of three young hearts on the Indian terrain and into the inner recesses of their souls, giving a new perspective to relationships, love and life.

Mohit is a successful entrepreneur for the past eleven years, running a successful conglomerate. He combined his love for travel, food and philosophy into this book.

ISBN: 978-93-82665-80-9; Price: 175/-; Pages: 200; Binding: Paperback.

Promise Me A Million Times
Keshav Aneel

Like a couple of migratory birds, both Charlie and Edwin leave to settle in the big city. For Edwin, it was to chase his dreams of becoming an actor; but for Charlie, it was just to be with his only friend.

Life throws Charlie in Aster's way. He could never have guessed, but he was in for an absolute unthoughtful phase of profoundness, which was going to last forever.

Keshav Aneel is a young marketing professional, who chose to do his heart's bidding and ended his brief corporate career to immerse himself into his creative side.

ISBN: 978-93-82665-73-1; Price: 175/-; Pages: 168; Binding: Paperback.

No Matter What I Do
Devanshi Sharma

Kabir, Amaira, Kushank and Suhani – four very different people bound together by love and friendship – are struggling to find the motto of their lives. Four threads entangled together and four lives recuperating each other – *No Matter What I Do* is the story of these four youngsters, on a journey to find themselves and how they reverse stereotypes on the way.

Devanshi Sharma is a twenty-one-year-old dreamer from Indore and strongly believes in hope. She enjoys talking, writing, dancing and eating, and her family is her lifeline.

ISBN: 978-9382665847; Price: 175/-; Pages: 200; Binding: Paperback.